MW01134140

Magus: Master of Martial Magic, Book I
The Magician's Primer
By Thomas Chilton Meseroll

<u>Eugene Burger</u>, On MAGIC magazine's list for being one of the most influential magicians of the twentieth century
"A fabulous tale incorporating Magic, Martial arts and Eastern Philosophy. I loved it! Tom Meseroll has managed to meld the many forms and philosophies of magic into a marvelous tale of good and evil."

<u>Sensei Jon Ochiai</u>, 3rd Dan Black-Belt Aikido and Movie Critic for IMDB
"Like the discipline of the martial arts, "Magus" is about surrender to the Path or the Way in one's own life. "Magus" embraces the wonder and surprise that is life through the transformational journey of Nicholas Thompson. "The Magus: Master of Martial Magic" is all about reclaiming and discovering one's greatness. That is the genesis of all true magic-- discovering one's own power and place in the universe. "Magus" has something for everyone. "Magus" is an allegory of mastery in life. Perhaps, true magic is about discovering one's own power, and enrolling others in their own inherent greatness. The power of the universe begins with being at one with it. The "Magus" explores these possibilities in an engaging, and entertaining tale of wonder and adventure."

<u>Scott Wells</u>, Society of American Magician's Book Review
"Remo Williams meets Mandrake the Magician!!..Not an overstatement that there is something for nearly everyone in this book..."

Meseroll, Thomas Chilton
Magus, Master of Martial Magic, Book 1, The Magician's Primer

***ISBN* – 978-1-4348-3057-9**

Magic Castle® used by permission Magic Castles Inc.

Previously released as a 500 copy Limited Edition Signed &
Numbered Hardbound at www.martialmagician.com

For Jill

All of the tricks within this novel exist; the real magic is within us all.

The secrets may be found on the pages that follow.

Chapter 1

Wonder is what sets us apart from other life forms. No other species wonders about the meaning of existence or the complexity of the universe or themselves.

Herbert W. Boyer

"Do you believe in Magic?"

"It is Magic that transports us back to a natural, infantile state of mind; a state of *Wonder*. As children, we *Wonder* at everything—the world is full of astonishment and mystery. Then, we learn how the world around us works and we lose that ability to be mystified with childlike awe. We lose our capacity for *Wonder* as our instincts have been dulled by our intellectual mind through years of study and practice."

"As you experience the magic today, revert back to your childlike-self; once again awaken your now dormant capacity for *Wonder*. Allow the awe and mystery of the universe to return. You will again be part of the enchantment, the mystery and the truly perceived reality of existence. You will, again ... believe."

There was a pause, as silence enveloped the pervading darkness.

"Let the Magic begin."

As these last words echoed through the lightless theater, the sound of wind chimes cut through the silence left by the finality of the phrase. This dark void and tintinnabulation delineated the perception of the senses in the theater.

However, this aura was only temporary because, unexpectedly, the darkness on the stage was interrupted by the appearance of two empty hands, lit from an unknown source, floating four feet above the floor. The disembodied hands turned over very slowly and then turned back with their palms towards the darkness above. The hands reached toward the audience revealing more arm in the light and produced (magically of course!) two very shiny, large, silver coins, one in each hand. The coins rested between the most distant ends of the thumbs and the index fingers as if they had been delicately pulled from the ether.

With the coins in their grasp, the hands began to move slowly forward into the illuminated space. The arms, and then the body of the magician, slowly appeared in the visible spectrum of the audience. He was a handsome man, tall, statuesque, with a goatee, wearing a black tuxedo with tails, crisp white shirt and bow tie. The Voice over the loudspeaker said, "Ladies and Gentleman, Nicholas Thompson, Magus, Master of Martial Magic!"

The applause was tremendous and continued throughout the theater as the magician raised the coins to his intensely focused eyes. He appeared to be looking beyond the audience, beyond the theater, towards a distant place in another time. The magician closed his eyes and positioned the coins over his closed lids.

The audience became silent.

Wind chimes tinkled gently as his hands leisurely dropped to his sides.

The focused circle of light on the stage expanded around him like the opening of the interlocking blades of a camera shutter. A beautiful young woman appeared in the slowly expanding wash of luminosity. In her hands were, what appeared to be, bandages for the injured, although as of yet we knew of no pain, nor dismemberment. Nevertheless, the evening was still young.

The attractive sorcerer's assistant gently placed two gauze eye patches over the silver coins on his eyes, and taped them securely on the magician's face. She raised her right hand and dropped an ace bandage with a flip of her wrist while keeping hold of one end, watching it expediently steam roll toward the floor, stopping one inch from the ground. The blinded magician remained at attention as she wrapped the bandage around his head and taped it in the back. He looked like a well-dressed casualty of war who had returned from battle, perhaps a battle of wizards, or perhaps an overly competitive headwaiter returning defeated from a cocktail tray-carrying contest at a local restaurant.

The assistant reached to the ground in front of the blinded magician and picked up a black satin bag. Casually she placed the bag over the magician's head and tied it with a cord around his neck. Now he appeared as a man about to be hanged. He had evolved from a war veteran to a well-dressed death row candidate. And yes, the evening was still young.

Attached to the magician's waist hung a scabbard, in all likelihood not noticed by the majority of the spectators. They were too busy watching the blinding-business with the eyes, or more likely, the misdirection caused by the beauty of the girl. However, as the magician's hand now grabbed the katana, the weapon of the Samurai, and extracted it with a flourish and a sound resembling a wet-stone against the blade of a knife, it was doubtful that anyone in the theater was still ignorant of the existence of the scabbard. In fact, an audible collective gasp rose from the audience as the katana was revealed.

The magician walked slowly forward on the stage while his assistant walked off into the wings. His heels "clicked" in the silence of the theater. The spotlight from above followed his motion and as he approached the front of the stage, the light revealed yet another beautiful woman, previously hidden in the darkness. Lying on a table, she wore a genie-like costume ala-Barbara Eden, bare tummy exposed. On this flat stomach there rested a watermelon, an unusual appendage to the beauty that lay beneath. An apple was held between her very white teeth. The apple pig for the barbecue was complete with a watermelon side dish ready to be sliced and served. And, yes, we would be getting to the slicing, very soon. However, it must be noted; the pig was no pig, but a fawn of perplexing beauty.

The magician slowly raised the sword above his head and halted in a statuesque tableaux preparing for a slice. The girl with the apple in her mouth, and watermelon on her stomach, appeared not to be breathing. Dust slowly settled down from the lights creating a faint appearance of snow flurries. The audience, like the girl, appeared not to be breathing as well. All was quiet. Patterns were captured, life was frozen and the theater particles were exactly where they were known to be by all, until…. the sword swung down with great speed reflecting photons from the spotlight creating a lightning flash throughout the theater. The sword made a vertical pass directly toward the girl's belly button (sorry Ms. Eden) slicing through the watermelon, pausing momentarily at the first layer of epidermis below the last line of atoms of watermelon, before drawing back up quickly. The sword returned to the position above the magician's head, but only for a second…. before he spun a full circle slicing horizontally across the length of the girl as he completed his spin. The sword passed an inch above her bare toes, her knees, her thighs, through the watermelon, over her breasts, and through the apple in her mouth. The top-half of the apple took flight into the air. The blindfolded magician completed his technique with the sword frozen in a position raised above his head, parallel to the floor. The top half of the apple was still floating in the air, the watermelon still together. All appeared to be in slow motion. As the apple reached its pinnacle, it seemed to slow down even more, and hang suspended in the air for a few seconds as the audience tried to catch their breath. As the apple began its descent to the floor, the four quarters of the watermelon, which had indeed been sliced, separated and fell off the girl as well. They all landed meat side down with a "splat."

The frozen moment lasted for a second before a tumultuous applause arose. The magician sheathed his sword with another flourish as the assistant from the wings returned to remove the bag from his head. She removed the bag and then the bandages. The magician then took the half dollar coins from his eyes and threw them into the air where they transformed into white doves. The birds flew over the audience, making a full circle of the theater before returning to the lovely arm of the standing assistant.

The applause became louder. It was to this ovation that the magician helped his genie assistant off the table. He removed the sliced apple half from her mouth and took a bite. Parenthesized by the two girls, he acknowledged the audience with a wink and a nod. They bowed in unison and the applause continued, as the black curtain dropped down restoring reality to the theater and to the minds of the audience.

However, as the tympani of hands receded, one figure remained sitting quietly, not moving but contemplating a magical world beyond the mayhem of the commotional crowd.

*   *   *

Pacific Ocean Park was a twenty-eight acre nautical-themed amusement park that had opened in 1958 at the Santa Monica Pier. It had intended to compete with Walt Disney's Disneyland in Anaheim. Among the twenty-six carnival-style attractions were two different fun-houses, The Flying Carpet, Sea Serpent Roller Coaster that extended beyond the pier over the ocean, Westinghouse Enchanted Forest, The Flying Dutchmen, Diving Bells, Ocean Skyway, 'Round the World in 80 Turns and the most popular ride, The Mystery Island Banana Train.

Although the P.O.P. attractions were sold off in 1976 to appease creditors after a Santa Monica urban renewal cut off pedestrian access and severely limited parking, the 1926 vintage Looff carousel from the original Santa Monica Pier remained.

Now the new Pier had Pacific Park with bumper cars, a Ferris wheel, arcade attractions and at the far end, a portable stage for entertainment. Two tall canvas-covered pole-strengthened flats formed an arch flanking either side of a stage. There was limited seating and standing room behind. This was the stage where *Magus, Master of Martial Magic* had just performed his stunning act.

As he exited the stage, Jen greeted Nicholas. She was equally handsome even though she was dressed all in black as a stagehand. She was holding the sword and placing it back into its travel box. The Entertainment director of the Pier came backstage. He was a young, energetic wanna-be film director.

"Wow! That was phenomenal! How did you do that?"

"Very carefully," smiled the tall, charming magician. "I sure do love being back here. Thanks for inviting us. It really takes me back. Do you remember when it was Pacific Ocean Park?" Nicholas queried the Entertainment director who shook his head, no.

"I remember coming as a child to P.O.P. My favorite exhibits were the House of Tomorrow where the 1939 World's Fair robot was still on display and the Flight to Mars. This was actually the place that inspired me to become an astrophysicist! A trip to outer space and especially to Mars always fascinated me as a kid. You know, to visit the little green Martians?"

The Entertainment director shrugged his shoulders with a sign of 'No Clue' what Nicholas was talking about.

"I guess you're too young," Nicholas sighed.

"Boy that sure dates you. I don't even remember that!" said Jen.

Nicholas blushed. "Ah, well, I was really young then, an aspiring astronaut."

Nicholas shook hands with the Entertainment director, "Thanks, tonight was fun." He rounded the flat and stepped down from backstage, leaving Jen to pack the props in a trunk.

*   *   *

The man who had remained behind as the audience had noisily exited to view the other attractions on the Pier sat quietly in his seat for a few moments with his eyes closed. Finally, he calmly opened them and softly he said aloud in his deep baritone voice, "It is time for the return of magic. It is time."

Chapter 2

*See first with your mind, then your eyes, and
finally with your body.*

Master Swordsman Yagyu Munenori

The white-crested dark waves rolled in large monolithic lines across the orange-red dawn horizon. To the north, as the shoreline curved west, lay the Santa Monica Mountains, original home of the Tongva and Chumash Indians, which was still a rare area of undeveloped woodland separating urban Los Angeles from the San Fernando Valley.

There were two magic hours in a day: one at dawn, the other at dusk, when rich hues from the sun occasionally reflected magnificently on the water. It was dawn now. The morning colors reflected off the dark sea in sparkles that begged to hear the reflected sound of wind chimes in unison with the light-dance they created upon the water. However, the beach was quiet and empty excluding the sound of the rumbling surf and a sole man who was dressed in a black karate hakama and a white GI top.

He was performing a Kata.

Kata, a series of pre-choreographed dance-like movements that resemble the slow focused motions of a Tai Chi master, only with speed, hardness and a sense of attack, as well as defense, is performed empty handed or with a weapon like a Nunchaku, Sai, or Bo. In this instance, the martial artist was using the nunchaku, two thick wooden batons about a foot long, attached to each other with rope at one end of each baton. He had two sets, one in each hand, each whirling about his head in a fluid but furious pace. From a distance, the flying sticks appeared to create an impregnable cocoon of force around his body---A Force-Field of Energy and Weaponry.

In the age of the samurai, nunchakus were common tools used by the peasants of Okinawa to till the soil before seeding. Nevertheless, just as desperate times called for desperate measures repeatedly throughout history, many new uses were found for common items, and so it was with the nunchakus. Long ago, when the peasants were not allowed weapons to defend themselves against the tyranny of the warlords, these farmers learned to use these tilling tools, called nunchakus, to protect themselves. Friederich Neitzche once said, "The slave is only noble when he revolts." In this case, not only was their act noble, but the Okinawan's revolt against oppression evolved into one of the most dignified and effective means of fighting, karate.

The man performing the feats of martial talent was the Magus: Master of Martial Magic, the magician from last night on the Pier. His name was Nicholas Thompson and he was indeed "The Magus" at night. This morning, however, the discipline was not magic, but focused training with meticulous precision. He completed his dance with the nunchakus and stopped with such intense restraint that it would appear he could stop the ocean itself from its motion. Nevertheless, the ocean, oblivious to Nicholas' routine, pounded the shore with thunderous waves. Nicholas was exhilarated and breathed in deeply. Every breath continued to enhance his spirit.

Nicholas found solace in the precise, repetitive kata technique he demonstrated. His training was his present, and was all he needed to know now. Kata utilized every muscle in his body, heightened his awareness of self and developed him into a formidable foe.

A lone seagull flew above the breaking waves in search of food, eyeing a school of small fish swimming through a wave as it peaked. The yellow-orange hue of the sky shone through the top of the wave as it broke revealing the darting shadows of the fish. They were engulfed beneath the water as another wave peaked and formed right behind the first. As this one rose, a much larger fish swam within. A great dark shadow followed the line of the wave. As it reached a crescendo, the large shark became visible, moving

9

horizontally across the water. Another wave peaked and broke while the shark swam downward beneath the water and disappeared before the crest reached the surface.

The magician stood frozen in a kata stance, staring at the surf. The next wave rose and there was no shark, no school of fish, no seagull, only wave and water. However, the ocean was and is a vast volume of water and waves, each wave contained something, jellyfish, seaweed, plankton or driftwood. Who can really say what was in each wave unless each wave was individually scrutinized at all times, for eternity? Who can really say that there is something in each wave, if the waves are not observed? A wave crashing in the surf, observed by no one, contains no water.

Nicholas for the most part lived in a perfect world – full of science, martial arts and magic, a perfect blending that created a most unique foundation of knowledge. Martial arts maintained his physicality, spirituality and focus. Magic allowed him to maintain a sense of wonder and to expand the limited minds of others to new heights through spectacular illusions and works of prestidigitation. Astrophysics allowed him to search for truth using a myriad of mathematical exercises and observations in search of the God Equation and solutions to riddles of the universe. Perfect. But, there was a missing variable or two in his equation of life recently, which he tried to keep deep beneath the surface of his reality.

Down the beach, two feet pounded toward the magician, occasionally sending a spray of sand granules flying. These bare feet were those of his beautiful young assistant and sister. She wore black sweat pants and a white t-shirt.

Nicholas continued to concentrate on the waves, oblivious to outside stimuli and ignored the approach of his sister and student of martial arts.

"Sorry I'm late," she said, panting out of breath, as she arrived at his side. "It was a late one last night. Had problems getting through the crowd to load the car. Excellent show though."

The magician relaxed his pose and looked slowly down toward her. He spoke quietly with determination and a sense of calm, "Thanks, they were a good audience. You were very helpful, but ..." he paused making a great circle with his arms pivoting while he looked toward the ocean, "... you should be here on time. Being late shows no respect. Training is important for everything you do in life. Timeliness shows dedication. Dedication brings results."

He had said his peace. She recognized he was scolding; it was something she had gotten used to. She loved her older brother, but she had never quite lived up to what she thought he considered her potential. She admired his constant determination to better himself and the world around him. For Nicholas, life was indeed not too short, but was perhaps just long enough for him to extract every experience and all knowledge out of everything he could, which would better his impact on the world and his understanding of the universe. This was his objective.

"There was a man who came backstage after the show last night. He was asking lots of questions about you and your performance." Nicholas put his nunchakus down gently in the sand, looked into his sister's eyes, and then toward the sea, and began a weaponless kata. He beckoned her to join, and soon they were synchronized in a mirror image of one another. Their universe for now was in the sand, and in their kata.

Seeing that there would be no response to her comment, she continued, "You'd already left, so I fended off the usual questions. But each question I answered seemed to escalate into more. I started getting very uncomfortable with his inquiries."

Still there was no response from Nicholas; it was as though he were not listening. He focused on his movements and stared at the sea.

She paused and continued, "That was what made me late ... well, that and not getting any sleep worrying about all his questions. He was an unusual man with an intense stare. Like he could see inside me."

11

Nicholas appeared to ignore her comments.

"You should always be on time for training. It is the most important thing we do," he said as he continued his techniques without a break.

They practiced their kata dance for another five seconds in silence before Nicholas asked, "So, what did he ask?"

"He said that you had surpassed the realm of ordinary magic," she said with bravado, trying to make up for being late by supplying his ego with a boost.

She added, "And that it appeared to the audience that you weren't doing tricks!"

"Uh-huh," he responded without inflection.

She continued with a few hand movements in sync with his and said, "He wanted to know where you came from and asked detailed questions about your martial arts background."

"So you told him, of course."

"I did," she replied, hesitantly, wondering if he was going to get angry.

"That is the objective, you know," he said, implying that she actually had an idea about what he was inferring to, which, of course, she did not.

Inquisitively, she questioned, "What *is* the objective?" Sometimes she just didn't understand him.

He paused in contemplation, and then after a deep breath, responded, "The objective of the true Magician is not to create a puzzle to be figured out. It is not to create curiosity and frustration, but to create mystery and awe, fill the observer with the euphoria of Wonder."

"Most often when a magician performs, the audience's minds become alive in trying to figure out what is happening and how the trick works. However, if the performer is very skillful, the method very well executed, the misdirection perfect, and the effect strong, then the minds of the audience stop trying to figure out the illusion and just feel awe and Wonder. It is at this point that they actually transcend their intellect."

"In the words of S.H. Sharpe, 'The key to the mysteries of the universe is "Wonder," and it is "Magic" that helps fabricate that key.' I do my best to open up the realm of possibilities, create the sense of Wonder and allow people to transcend their limited beliefs."

He paused and then pointed out, "*That* is the objective."

"So that would make you Mr. Wonderful!" she responded with a touch of humor.

"Ah, my sister ... forever the muse," he smiled slightly. "I do my best sis." He took a very slight verbal pause to correct her arm position in one of the training moves she held, and then said, "And Jen, what did you tell this inquisitive man?"

"Oh, the usual of course," she said blandly, as if she had recited this a million times before.

"You studied Okinawan weaponry for twenty-some odd years; you are a black belt in Shotokan Karate, a Tai Chi Master, and a juggler extraordinaire. You have been performing magic since you were a wee lad of five. You have a Ph.D. in Astrophysics and teach at the University in the Astronomy department."

And then sarcastically she added, "I failed to mention your crocheting, though, is that okay?"

"Fine. Then don't expect an Afghan blanket under your Christmas tree," he replied glibly. They paused momentarily in their techniques to smile while they looked at each other. But, Jen looked strained.

"He seemed to want to know more about you than anyone else who has come backstage after one of your shows ... Maybe I told him too much." Her late arrival to the training session had been all but forgotten, and the sun now climbed higher in the sky.

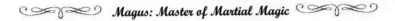

Their smiles diminished and they resumed their martial attitudes.

Nicholas spoke one final time, "Not to worry. You told him nothing that he couldn't have gotten searching the net ... we need to focus on our training, then on tonight's show at the Magic Castle. I've got a class this afternoon, too." His hand began to make a slow circular motion in front of his body. His sister started off behind and then quickly synchronized her circular movements with his. The circular motions of their hands continued as the waves stormed the beach. There was much Wonder on the horizon not yet realized, and although the day was new, the technique was old, and the practitioners were just temporally passing through.

Chapter 3

*Anyone who is not shocked by quantum theory,
has not understood it.*

Niels Bohr

The circular motion of the martial magician's hand on the blackboard was performed with the same finesse and ease of motion as his kata performance, as he erased the integrals and differential equations from the imitation slate. These were the equations, which attempted to solve the mysteries of the universe, but of course, in the classroom, the majority of the participants missed this minute detail. By removing them from the board, only the black void, which underlies all, prevailed. As the chalk dust adhered to the eraser fibers, the martial artist was no longer in training; the magician was no longer on stage. Instead, he was the professor of astrophysics in a university astronomy classroom, and right now, this was all that concerned the students.

Students of astrophysics were of a different breed. Some of them assumed the appearance of the well-defined nerd complete with pocket protectors and calculators. Many however, deviated from from the curve of the typical. Some, like the famous Richard Feynman, played bongos and hung out in seedy bars during off-hours. Others rode in motorcycle gangs or rock-climbed impossible pinnacles in Brazil. There was no standard look or persona for an astrophysicist. The only required criterion for success was to have the problem-solving capacity of a super computer, while possessing the mathematical insight of an autistic idiot savant. Bongo playing was just a perk.

Nicholas, of course, thrived in this the norm. There was a plethora of outcasts world of the non-conformity allowance plan. In his professorial capacity, he assumed the persona of the nerdy professor. On this occasion, he was wearing his jeans, brown top-siders, dark green corduroy jacket with brown suede patches on the elbows, and a black polo shirt. He liked dressing the part of a professor. He filled the role admirably. His spectacles were representative of those owned by the Ben Franklin sect, which completed his ensemble, making him a member in good standing to the Council of Geeks. As on the magical stage or on the martial artist's beach, he was equally at home in this collegiate environment.

He had erased most of the mathematical equations from the blackboard, leaving a few untouched, perhaps for future inquiries. There was a laptop and mouse on a table off to the side of the blackboard. The laptop was connected to a projector. Nicholas walked over to the projector, turned it on and immediately an animated image of a wall with two slits appeared on a white movie screen off to the side of the black board. The students turned toward the screen. In physics, this image was known as the *Two-Slit Experiment*, for obvious reasons (two slits in a wall). The image on the screen was a two-dimensional wall as seen from above, with two slits, or gaps, in the structure. And although the slits were very close together, their separation was discernable. Pointing towards the wall from the left side of the screen was a cartoon cannon.

Nicholas casually clicked an icon on the computer screen with his mouse and a steady stream of cannon balls proceeded to bombard the cartoon wall. Some balls passed through the two slits as they succumbed to the voids in the barrier. These animated balls, the students knew, represented particles, being fired at the slits. The particles that actually did pass through the slits formed a distinctive pattern of lines on a wall some distance past the slits, on the right side of the screen. Rorschach would have had a blast with the psychoanalysis of the patterns. A cartoon-blinking eye was off to the side of the screen watching the action, most likely trying to discern whether the blobs of collided particles were a stabbing, a wooly mammoth or a sexual fantasy, ala Rorschach.

Professor Thompson looked up towards the animated screen, then back to his class of undergraduate physics students, and continued his lecture, "So, the 'Two-Slit Experiment' shows us that when many particles are fired towards two slits they have an equal probability of going through either slit."

He paused as he pointed to the stream of particles going through the slits. Although his speech pattern was not as entertaining as when he was on stage, conjuring, it was still rather theatrical. He was definitely interested in the subject matter, which was half the battle for a teacher.

He pointed again toward the screen, "And these dots, of course, interact on the other side, like waves with nodal lines which are void of dots in between."

There did in fact appear to be a pattern in the chaos of the blobs. (The dots were grouped together in vertical columns, like the slats of a picket fence, with larger slats in the middle tailoring off to thinner slats towards the outskirts of the wall.)

"BUT if we send just one particle towards the two slits," he clicked on the mouse eliminating the exodus of particles and fired just one particle towards the slits. It moved very slowly across the screen, towards the slits.

The students followed the cannon ball projectile along with the blinking eye on the screen.

"And with determination, we do not try to establish which slit the dot is passing through . . ."

The particle was still approaching the slits as he "clicked" the mouse one more time and deleted the Rorschach searching blinking eye.

"It will actually pass through both slits and interact with itself on the other side."

The students saw the particle approaching the two slits and then as it hit right between them, it changed into a wave pattern and proceeded through both slits. It then interacted with itself as two sets of waves on the other side of the slits. As it hit the far wall, it formed a pattern of blobs, similar to what had been seen when the multitudes of dots were fired.

The majority of the students did not seem impressed. Perhaps a Spiderman cartoon would have been a better choice for this audience.

"Does anyone know the implications of this experiment?" Nicholas was trying to break the obviously un-awed audience silence.

About thirty-percent of the class raised their hands. A few actually looked like they were interested, and some just wanted to impress the Professor by attempting to answer the question.

Nicholas chose Michael for a response. Michael was not the sharpest tool in the shed, or in class, or at home, or anywhere else for that matter. Maybe this once, he thought, Michael had an epiphany.

"Yes, Michael. What do you suspect is the implication?" he said, actually suspecting that the right answer would come from elsewhere in the room.

"Modern psychology is wrong," he said trying to impress the women with his 'better than thou' attitude towards Professor Thompson.

"There really are split personalities!"

This did in fact produce a few giggles from his less intelligent classmates.

"Thank you Sybil and Michael," responded Dr. Thompson, knowing that only one-percent of the class would recognize the name Sybil as the most severely documented split personality case in history, and out of that one-percent, one-hundred percent probably only knew this because of the movie with Sally Fields. Thank God for television. Where would our knowledge base be without the high-speed beam of electrons that fly through a vacuum and hit the flat phosphor coated screen to form the image we call TV? And what if the beam of electrons in our TV had to go through two slits? 'Hmmm ...,' he thought.

The Professor continued, "But truthfully, in a way Michael, you are correct."

Michael was confused. How could he be correct? Oh no, he thought, perhaps it was a set-up where his true ignorance would be revealed.

The Professor realized his advantage and continued, "In fact, each particle has two personalities. A wave personality, which allows the one particle to go through both slits, and a particle personality, which it collapses into or becomes, if we try to observe which slit it will go through."

The classroom was trying to keep up. Michael was definitely lost.

"Kind of cool, huh?" Professor Thompson said with a smirk.

The class looked a bit bewildered, but was still intrigued, especially since it appeared that Michael had provided some fodder for the Professor.

Now that the class had returned to his domain and their attention was back, Nicholas continued, "Let's try the single particle experiment again."

He clicked the mouse again. The screen refreshed and erased the previous blobs. A single particle began to move slowly toward the slits, "But this time, let's add the observer back in." He clicked the mouse again and the blinking eye returned.

"Now watch as the particle remains a particle and passes through only one slit and indeed, does not form a pattern on the other side."

The students watched the dot move across the screen as the blinking eye blinked and the slits awaited contact. The particle approached one slit and passed through. The eye blinked and the particle continued on its merry way as a dot and painted a single-point blob against the wall.

"You see it truly is the act of observation which collapses the wave form into the solid particle!" the Professor exclaimed with much enthusiasm.

Another hand arose quickly from the back of the class. This hand was connected to a much brighter student. He spoke as his hand arrived at its apex.

"So if all particles are also waves when not observed, what is the relationship between everything when no one is looking?"

The student paused and then continued, "Is everything like one big ocean of waves?"

The Professor looked down toward the floor in contemplation and then responded as he looked up, "You are absolutely correct! It is like one big ocean. However, it is even more closely tied together than the Chaos theory example of the butterfly flapping its wings in Tokyo causing the tidal wave in California. It is much more tightly intertwined. Much more."

The Professor again contemplated the infinite and then continued, "You see at the quantum level there is what Einstein called *a spooky interaction over distance*. Related particles actually know that they are being measured or observed instantaneously regardless of the spatial distance between them. A particle in New York instantaneously becomes aware of its counterpart, or as we call it, entangled particle, if it is being measured in China."

Some students were just in awe and some at this point were just ignorant. In fact, it was difficult to recognize the differences between the two types in the faces of the students.

"At the quantum level it is like one big infinite ocean, where everything is related, and everything has the potential of being influenced by everything else. It is the act of observation that causes the ocean-universe of waves to break down and actually become particles."

More confusion and mystery appeared on the students' faces.

He continued anyway. "But without observation, it would seem that everything is all part of the same ocean or energy force and in that primeval jambalaya everything interacts with everything else and everything is part of the whole ocean of existence."

He paused for effect and then said with emphasis one more time, "Every particle and every being interacts, impacts, and has the potential to influence, or be it, control, every other particle within this ocean of existence."

The silence held the class at bay for a moment.

No one really knew what to say. Some were too confused while others actually understood the implications of the theory, which confused them even more.

So, the professor, the magician, the martial artist concluded the class with emphasis.

"Sort of cool, huh?" he asked as the bell rang.

Chapter 4

> *The more important secrets of the Magic art have been known but to few, and those few have jealously guarded them, knowing that the more closely they concealed the clue to their mysteries, the more would those mysteries be valued.*

Professor Hoffman

The Magic Castle was an icon in the magical community. It was also the clubhouse for the Academy of Magical Arts. Magic Castle historian and biographer, Carol Marie, wrote, "The Magic Castle sprang from the ruins of many architectural treasures found in California and Europe to become a unique Hollywood lair for actors, performers and prestidigitators alike. Decorated with memorabilia from the world's greatest magicians, it maintained a strong connection to the elite of Hollywood. The Magic Castle became the Mecca of magic and a most desirable place to visit. Apparitions of conjurors from long ago could be felt in the richly paneled halls and lurking in dark corners watching... watching.... waiting for that next grand illusion."

"The turreted mansion itself was an enigmatic illusion, being four times larger on the inside than it appeared from the outside. Built into the Hollywood hillside, the most eastern point of the Santa Monica Mountains, the gothic structure had faded into oblivion in the mid-twentieth century before being resurrected into the world's most exclusive private magic restaurant club. The Magic Castle was truly a premier international magic institution and unique museum, library and theatrical establishment."

The Victorian mansion, which was to become the Magic Castle, was built in 1908 and was restored complete with its richly appointed interior in the early 1960's by Milt Larsen, co-founder of the Academy of Magical Arts.

It served as a 'Members Only' retreat for magicians to mingle, perform and to share their secrets of magic. They could study the Magical Arts in a legendary library of books, instruction manuals, and lecture notes housed in the lower labyrinth of the manor as well as from each other, in a true brotherhood of magic. It was an exclusive club where magician members auditioned (and then, of course, paid dues) to join. Magicians around the world dreamt of one day presenting their own brand of magical mysteries at the Magic Castle while visitors schemed to obtain an invitation to this wondrous clubhouse. Only open to the public for dinner and shows by personal invitation from a member, it was possible to see as many as eight or ten magicians performing every evening.

The showrooms within included a Close-up Gallery, a large theatre known as the Palace of Mystery, and the Parlor of Prestidigitation for intimate stand-up magic. There were five cocktail lounges located throughout, and in one, a grand piano where a talented ghost played requests or answered questions musically. The Magic Castle was THE place for a magician to get booked and was the perfect place for Nicholas to showcase his new act in the Palace of Mystery.

The darkness of night enhanced the beauty of the luminous aura that surrounded the Magic Castle. Elegantly dressed and coiffed patrons entered the lobby of the three-story Victorian mansion and patiently waited to confirm their reservations and enter. To the left of the large gothic beveled doors that opened into the lobby, a lit marquis revealed the prestidigitators who would entertain that evening. Tonight it read:

"Don Wilt" - Close-Up Gallery

"Anthony Blake" - Parlor of Prestidigitation

"The Magus: Master of Martial Magic"-

Palace of Mystery, the Grand Auditorium

(8:30 & 10:30)

Before entering the club, all members and guests passed through the lobby, which at first glance, appeared to be a small room with only one door – the entrance door. There was a fireplace and shelves full of dusty old books along the walls, presumably arcane books of magic. A receptionist greeted the guests from behind a large desk and validated either membership or a member's invitation. After verification of credentials, she gave the instructions and password to enter the true entrance to the Magic Castle. By facing the owl statuette that sat on one of the dusty bookshelves and declaring the magical password, the entire bookshelf slid to the left, revealing a hallway that led to the magical labyrinth beyond where magic flowed in abundance.

Two nattily attired men approached the owl. "So you've never seen The Magus perform?" asked the younger gentleman of the two. When the grey-haired older man nodded in confirmation, the younger one continued. "All I know about him is his real name is Nicholas Thompson and he is just unbelievable. It is my understanding that the other magicians don't even know how he does what he does. They are shocked and amazed as much as the general public. He is known as the Master of Martial Magic, and to tell you the truth, I think his magic is more mystical than magical. He seems to have some uncanny ability." He continued jokingly, "He may well be a Jedi Knight."

The older gentleman responded in his best Obi-wan Kenobi voice, "Use the Force Luke." They laughed and then turned to the awaiting owl, and said in unison, "Open Sesame."

The wall of books slid to the left and the two gentlemen passed into another world, a world of mystery and magic. They were prepared to see some of the most mystifying effects, not only on the stage, and not only by the paid magicians, but moreover throughout the catacomb-like halls of this magical society. One never knew what you would find at the Magic Castle.

Eager to see The Magus, the two gentlemen climbed their way up the stairs to the large stage theatre and joined the other patrons in the Palace of Mystery's waiting area. They stepped in line and were delighted that one of the Castle's docent tour guides, Carol Marie, was expounding about Chung Ling Soo in the hallway.

"Chung Ling Soo, also known as William Ellsworth Robinson, represented in four posters on the walls here, was a very unique self-promoter. He would book himself into a theatre and challenge the local art students to design a poster for his show. He printed very limited quantities of the winning entry poster, making them very rare and therefore very valuable to magic poster collectors around the world. The Magic Castle is proud owner of five of these posters, the four here and one in the Grand Salon area at the entrance. Chung Ling Soo had a wonderful and exciting life until 1918 when, unfortunately he perished on stage from a faulty 'catch the bullet in the mouth' illusion. You didn't know that Magic could be very dangerous..." She led her group down the hallway toward the Parlor as the Palace of Mystery opened its doors.

The theatre began to fill and quickly reached its capacity. There was an edge of anticipation and excitement in the air. The black curtain on stage was drawn, hiding the potential secrets behind its veil of velvet.

"Ladies and Gentlemen, the Magic Castle is proud to present, The Magus, Master of Martial Magic!"

With an unusual Asian musical fanfare, the curtain opened to reveal Nicholas Thompson, The Magus, as he stood in the spotlight center stage, completely still, holding an ornate samurai sword over his head.

It was the same katana sword as the night before, but this time there were no ladies provocatively dressed to distract from his performance. There was only the magician in the limelight, wearing black pants and a black sleeveless silk shirt. He stood, as any Iado master would, in this martial arts pose; a pose originated from the samurai in preparation for slicing a threat in half: a human threat. The Magus was serious. Very serious.

After only the briefest moment, The Master of Martial Magic began to make very slow dance-like moves, cutting through the air with his sword, in a samurai-style kata dance. During an appropriate pause in the music, The Magus held the katana in front of his waist, and as the music slowly began to increase in volume, he threw the sword away from his hands and let go ....

The sword floated in the air in front of his body, apparently hanging in the air by some mysterious force. He danced to the music and in a parallel Ginger and Fred-style movement, the sword danced with him. The large gilt handle represented a head, and the blade a body, and it began to float around The Magus in synchronized motion. He performed an entire dance routine with the floating sword. It was a phenomenal illusion and his cat-like dance movements held the audience's attention, but with the additional mystery of the floating, dancing sword, it really suspended their understanding of reality beyond comprehension.

Finally, after a huge crescendo, the music came to an end as the sword flew up in the air in front of him and he caught it by the handle. He bowed as the applause became deafening.

Nicholas waved to subdue the applause but to no avail. So instead, he reached behind his back and grabbed a second sword. The applause dwindled as the understanding awakened. Again, he made slow movements with the swords, as in a kata. Again, he released the swords in front of his body, only this time there were two. The swords both floated and proceeded to dance around his persona in sync as he performed Tai Chi motions with his hands.

Suddenly, the music stopped, and the swords hovered, frozen in time and space in front of his body. The swords slowly lowered point to the ground, handle in the air, as The Magus began to float off his feet and rotate slowly towards the swords. He grabbed the handles in both hands while his legs and feet floated up into a perfect handstand, on top of the two swords. The applause continued as he flipped forward with the swords in his hands and landed on his feet, the swords crossed over his head.

The black curtain dropped and the house lights faded up, once again thrusting the audience into the reality of the theater. The applause seemed like it might never end but inevitably the hands began to tire and the clapping subsided in a slow diminuendo.

As the audience began to leave there was a single man left behind. He was a large man, perhaps Middle Eastern, perhaps African, or perhaps Samoan. He had a mostly grey beard and white hair. He wore loose-fitting clothes and had adopted, or borrowed, a tight-fitting sports jacket for the evening. It was obviously not his natural choice of attire. He looked out of place in his clothes, but at the same time, he looked very comfortable and confident in his demeanor. He stared at the stage and said quietly in a melodic deep voice, "It is time for the education of The Magus."

*   *   *

The dressing rooms at the Magic Castle were on the small side, although they may have been the best in the magic community. They were the best for the majority of the performers who visited once or twice a year. However, for the premiere world-renown performers, there were larger dressing rooms with a bit more room and nicer amenities. This was to allow for the quiet preparation or meditation, which occurred before a performance, or even for a brief rehearsal in front of a mirror between shows. In the case of the Magus, his dressing room was, indeed, one of the larger ones. His performances brought many return patrons and thus larger profits. Practice, of course, makes perfect, or at least the appearance of perfection, which was the resolve of the true conjuror. And so, Nicholas continually practiced.

The dressing room and back stage noises faded away as the stagehands and fellow performers disappeared for sustenance and libations. The next performance would not be for another hour. Jen and the other assistant had left for dinner. Nicholas was juggling. The large Arabian knives that flew in front of his face were for concentration, focus, and the evolution of a new trick he was working on. Shiny reflections sparkled off the chrome blades, telegraphing a deadly threat. And they were threatening. The Magus juggled the large sabers over his head, in front of his face, as he lay supine on a table in the middle of his dressing room. Each knife spun three hundred sixty degrees in the air once before he caught the handle. He focused on the symmetry of the pattern and the consistency of his handling as the knives flew through the air, shimmering in a quick flurry of metal and hands. The slightest slip could have caused a mortal injury, knocking him in the head or stabbing him in the throat or eye. There was silence in his dressing room except for the sound of his hands slapping against the wooden handles as he grabbed the spiraling knives.

Focus was the key.

Nothing could disturb his concentration ... nothing ... not even the knock at the door, heard by him, but ignored as the knives continued flying. He responded to nothing but their movement.

There was another knock.

"Come in," responded Nicholas finally, as he continued to juggle the knives. He did not intend to stop now. The husky, dark man from the theater entered. He cautiously approached the far end of the table and watched the flying blades as they rotated in the air.

Nicholas did not falter from his juggling and remained silent. There was no need for discourse as far as Nicholas was concerned. The act of juggling was more than enough to keep him occupied. His triceps were certainly at a point of no return.

The mystery man began, "Mr. Magus, I wanted to commend you in person for your marvelous performances, both last night and tonight. You truly are an amazing man."

The knives continued to fly in front of the magician's face as he responded, "Call me Nicholas, and thank you. I assume you are the man who spoke with my sister last night as well."

"You are correct, Nicholas. My name is Ahura, and in my land, I too, am a magician of a sort. I am known as a Magi."

"Magi?" questioned Nicholas.

28

"Yes, Magi," the large man responded as he bowed his head.

"Ah, the Magi. Truly?" said Nicholas with some suspicion. Knives were still flying, his eyes never blinked. "That is, of course, where I got my stage namesake from."

Silence beckoned in the room, so Nicholas continued.

"I believe the original Magus was Zoroaster, and weren't the three Wiseman known also as Magi? The ones that found the baby Jesus?"

"Yes, they were of the Magi sect," said Ahura. "The Magi, as you probably know, originated in Persia. And yes, one of the first Magi was Zoroaster. He was known as the Magus, the derivation from which your words Magic and Magician originate. But I am sure you already know all of this."

"But I thought the Magi and Zoroasterism was an extinct sect? Where are you from?" Nicholas questioned, as he began to get curious. The knives continued to fly.

Ahura responded knowingly, "There still is a small group of Zoroasterists, but for the most part, they have been smothered by political oppression. However, the Magi have continued to practice for many centuries in seclusion, which brings me to why I wanted to talk to you." Ahura's eyes stared intently at the magician awaiting the response.

"Thanks for the little history lesson, but I really do have to practice a little more before the second show tonight," he said, dodging the request of his guest. "But you know, maybe you could do me a favor before you leave. You see that deck of cards fanned out on the counter in front of you?" he asked while carefully nodding his head to the fanned out deck on the makeup counter by Ahura's hands, while the knives still spun in front of his so far, unblemished face.

Ahura looked at the deck and then back towards Nicholas.

"Yes."

"Pick a card from the pack, look at the card, memorize it, put it back in the pack, pick up the whole deck and place it in your right hand," Nicholas said, sounding like the performer and the magician, not a dressing room host.

Ahura picked a card from the middle of the pack, glanced at the card and then placed the card back into the pack. He then promptly picked up the whole deck and placed it in his right hand. He was very nimble and adept for a man of his large stature. His hands moved with the fluidity and poise of a ballet dancer.

Nicholas was still juggling. The knives never faltered from their paths above his head. He slowly sat up as Ahura finished with the cards. He was still juggling, and the knives were now in front of his body as he sat on the side of the table.

Nicholas caught one of the knives in his right hand and pointed with it to a white board resting on a stand, about three feet in front of where he sat. As he continued to juggle the other two in his left hand, he said, "Throw the deck of cards towards the white board in front of me at the count of three."

Ahura looked at the white board. The knives resumed their movements in their familiar configuration with both hands juggling, while Nicholas shouted, "ONE...TWO...THREE!"

Ahura threw the deck of cards in the air toward the white board. As the cards fluttered in the air, Nicolas grabbed one knife in mid-flight and pulled it back over his shoulder only to throw it directly into the fluttering cards. The other two knives were still flying in front of his face. The thrown knife turned over once in the air and nailed one card to the white board face-out towards Nicholas and Ahura. As the knife hit the white board with a loud thud, Nicholas caught the other two knives and froze in motion.

The rhythmic sound of the juggling ceased and the dressing room became silent, except for the last of the cards, fluttering to the ground.

As Nicholas turned slowly towards Ahura, he asked, "Is that your card?" Penn and Teller would have been so proud of his delivery of that question.

Ahura walked slowly over to the white board. He nonchalantly looked at the card and saw that it was, indeed, the card that he had picked from the deck. He nodded and said, "Jack of Diamonds. Correct."

Nicholas smiled. He was now in control again. He knew much better than to let an opponent get the advantage, or at least, that was his current perception.

"I do love getting it right, and sometimes ... Well, you just never know," he said, knowing perfectly well that he got it right more often than not.

"Ah, but the true Magi does always know," said Ahura with confidence, as he walked away from the white board, leaving the card and knife intact.

Nicholas realized he had left an opening in their conversation.

"He knows because he is totally aware of everything around him and within. True Magic is control of what is without, by understanding that it is all, truly, within. By learning this you can do real Magic."

Nicholas stared, actually beginning to listen to this strange man as Ahura continued.

"Let me give you an example. Think of a card, any card. Do not tell me what it is, but empty your mind of all thoughts and concentrate on that card alone. Will you give it a try?"

Nicholas nodded once yes, and appeared to be concentrating very hard. Martial arts focus. His eyes were open as Ahura said, "So are you focused on the card in your mind?"

Nicholas nodded, "Yes."

Ahura's hand gently brushed against his pant leg, as if he was moving an invisible object off his leg. As his hand moved across his pants, the card beneath the knife blade on the white board appeared to change from the Jack of Diamonds to a blank white card. Just as suddenly, it transformed into the Ten of Spades.

"Is that your card?" said Ahura, impressing not only the spirits of Penn and Teller, but Nicholas, and God as well.

Nicholas stared at the white board bewildered and said quietly, "Yes." He removed the knife from the ten of spades and looked at it, front and back. Nicholas looked back to the strange man. He was obviously dumbfounded and no longer in control, so the Magi continued, "You see, the true magician knows that reality is based on your perception. A wise man once said: *Your focus determines your perception, which in turn determines your reality.* True magic is based on this premise."

Nicholas remained perplexed and for a rare moment appeared not to know what to say. Confounded and needing to understand, he finally said, "Perhaps you would like to sit and have some tea?"

"Perhaps," said Ahura.

*　　　　*　　　　*

The Tea Ceremony in Japan is a formal ritual very similar to the routines of kata in martial arts, where every movement is precise, pre-ordained and purposeful. The tea sharing ceremony, which Nicholas Thompson and Ahura were performing, was also precise and purposeful although the pre-ordained aspect was yet to be determined. Its purpose, for Nicholas, was to understand Ahura's mysterious identity, and if possible, ascertain the precise methods, which allowed him to perform such a miraculous feat of magic moments ago in the magician's dressing room. Such magic was sacrilege, to fool a magician in his own magical dressing room.

It should be a capital violation against the magician's code of ethics. Nevertheless, ethical or not, there was a teapot between the two magicians, and the sharing of the tea and the discourse that followed absolved all.

They were facing each other at the table as Nicholas took a sip of his tea. He was staring at Ahura over his cup as he said, "So, who are you again?"

Ahura sipped his tea as he looked up from his cup.

"I am known as Ahura Mazda in my land, as I said before. I have been called the wise one, and I am here to instruct you in the ways of the Magi."

Nicholas responded quickly in the anticipation of learning a new trick, "You mean instruct me in what you just did? Well sir, that was pretty impressive. I'd love to learn how you did that." Nicholas started to hand him a deck of cards.

Ahura held his hand up and responded calmly, "It is not that easy."

"I'll bet," said the magician, now beginning to see that Ahura might not be so forthcoming.

Ahura continued, "You see, I have been following your career from afar for some time Dr. Thompson, and you have some very special talents. I think your studies of science, magic, and martial arts have helped you evolve into much more than you are aware. In addition, there are your own natural abilities. There is a reason for everything, including your inherent talents as well as those that you have cultivated into something more. All of this and much more is what will be required for your future education. And it is based on your heritage, your gene-pool so to speak, which makes it absolutely imperative, for the preservation of "life" as you know it, that you allow me to train you in the ways of the Magi."

Still wondering whether he would be learning the trick tonight, and appreciating the compliment, Nicholas responded, "Thank you very much, but you see, even with all these compliments and all my intellectual capacities, I still have no idea how you did that last trick with the card."

Ahura shook his head and said, "But you see, that is just it: It was not a trick. It was, in fact, the true definition of magic, as the word is derived from the word MAGI. It was the Magi who performed feats such as this, and it is from their example that today's magic is based. This magic was an exercise of my will, its effect on what is perceived and how things interact. This is true magic."

Nicholas was still puzzled, and wondered whether this was part of an act. It was a damn good act if it was.

Ahura continued, "I understand this is all a bit new, but these are truths of which you are very much aware. If I recall correctly, a few years back you submitted a letter to one of the physics journals entitled, 'Quantum Perceptions.' You said, and I quote as best I can, 'At the quantum level all of reality is but a probability. These probabilities become truths depending on the perspective of the observer. Perspective therefore determines reality, and it is your focus, that determines your perspective. The will controls your ability to focus. Thus by developing the will, you can control your reality'."

Nicholas acknowledged the hypothesis, "So, you've been doing your homework. I am very impressed. But that was written a while back, and you know what? I was mocked for those concepts." He was obviously sensitive to the subject. "So, I actually stopped pursuing those thoughts. Now you are saying that you used your will to change my perception of what just happened." His disbelief was unbounded.

Aura continued, "I am saying that I used my will to influence your perception of reality. By studying the way of the Magi, you shall learn to control reality as well. You will learn how the universe is interconnected with all life-force in an infinite sea of possibilities and how to influence the waves within that sea."

He paused while this set in and then continued, "It is because of your background and your natural talents that I think it would behoove you to take a sabbatical from your efforts here and come with me for a few months to begin learning the ways of the MAGI."

"And where is that?" asked Nicholas with curiosity and puzzlement.

"The Karakoram Mountain Range that borders China, Afghanistan, Pakistan, and Russia. That is where the MAGI have lived for over 2000 years. That is where we must go."

Chapter 5

The universe is a unified whole that can to some extent be divided into separate parts, into objects made of molecules and atoms, themselves made of particles. But here, at the level of particles, the notion of separate parts breaks down. The subatomic particles—and therefore, ultimately, all parts of the universe—cannot be understood as isolated entities, but must be defined through their interrelations.

Henry Stapp

Forty-five miles west of Washington D.C., entombed beneath eighty-five acres of solid impregnable rock was the cavernous underground city known as Mount Weather. In the event of nuclear warfare or other major disaster, this was where the elite civilians and the top government and military officials would seek shelter. There was even a secret list of those who would have a 'ticket' to the after-world party. This special facility was run by the Federal Emergency Management Agency (FEMA)--not the obvious choice of covert government organizations. The Mount Weather facility, though, was not just another fallout shelter; it was an underground city complete with roads, sidewalks, a battery powered-subway, office buildings, cafeterias, dormitories and apartments, and of course a state-of-the-art hospital. There was an artificial lake that shimmered from the glow of fluorescent lights. It had its own internal water and power, food storage to last for a century, and a "bubble-shaped pod" that housed the most advanced computer known to civilization. However, the most interesting facet of Mount Weather had to do with its full-time residents.

There was a duplicate U.S. government within the subterranean city. Undisclosed persons there mimicked the responsibilities of the elected leaders, making Mount Weather an eerie doppelganger of the United States of America. A wing known as "The White House" housed the President. There was a cabinet to the President complete with a secretary of Agriculture, Commerce, Health, Housing and Urban Development, Interior, Labor, State, Transportation and the Treasury. Protocol even demanded that the underground president be known as "Mr. President" and the cabinet members went by Mr. or Ms. Secretary. Hundreds of employees lived beneath the granite mountain full-time.

The underground bunker also included a crematorium, dining and recreation areas, sleeping quarters, reservoirs of drinking and cooling water, an emergency power plant, and a radio and television studio, which was part of the Emergency Broadcasting System. A series of side-tunnels accommodated twenty office buildings, some of which were three stories tall. There was an on-site ninety-thousand gallon/day sewage treatment plant. Although the facility was designed to accommodate several thousand people, only the President, the Cabinet, and Supreme Court were provided private sleeping quarters.

Dr. Burton Carrier was a mole. Or at least that was *his* interpretation of his life for the past eight years. Tall and skinny, with a receding hairline, he already looked older than his thirty-two years. The white lab coat was his uniform of choice. It covered a multitude of sins, but they were hidden beneath his pristine cleanliness. His personal grooming, the placement of his pens in his pockets and even which side of the white board the eraser was placed was of utmost importance to him. His time was spent focusing on resolving the order of the universe, and in his world, he was in complete control. 'Anal' would be an understatement in regards to his association with the universe around him.

It takes a certain personality to live underneath the ground for years, never seeing natural sunlight or feeling the wind or rain on their skin. Burton had surfaced to the top of terra firma only a handful of times in the eight years he had been assigned to Mount Weather, and during these trips, he had only gone as far as the nearby town of Bluemont. There were more conveniences underground at Mount Weather than there were in Bluemont. He liked it underground and didn't want to leave. He had been recruited right out of the Ph.D. program at Cal Tech to delve into the mysteries of the universe, from his post, far beneath the known world.

It was ironic. He studied the complexities of the universe from a site where he was blind to the heavens. His mole-like existence was a double-edged sword; he was a burrowing animal that lived beneath the ground and he was an undercover spy. His work though, opened up more of heaven and the mind of God than the visual cosmos ever would, and he did it from a hell-hole beneath the earth.

And this was his ultimate goal in life, because ...

Burton Carrier wanted to be God.

He was a black mamba amongst the naïve worms and garter snakes of the scientific community. Albeit there may have been a few political rattlesnakes amongst the world of physicists, none had the venom and drive of Burton Carrier.

His experiments in physics gave him the privilege of delving into the mind of God and peeking at the secrets of creation. This was why he worked beneath the ground supported by government funds. Not for the advancement of the U.S. government, nor the advancement of science. He performed his experiments for the advancement of Burton Carrier. He not only wanted to peek behind the veil of the Almighty, he wanted to be the Almighty. And 'God'-forbid that anyone got in his way.

Of course, Burton had been courted by the CIA, not because of his quest to become God, but instead because of his studies in Quantum Entanglement and Cryptography. The CIA had many smaller compartmentalized agencies, such as this, the Advanced Intelligence Agency (AIA), housed in a special wing-town of the Mount Weather underground city. This agency seemed to fit Burton's skills the best, for his quantum physics prowess, as well as his somewhat anti-social behavior. It was here that Burton worked and lived.

Quantum Entangled particles allowed the instantaneous communication of information, theoretically at large distances, even at infinity. By measuring one quantum-entangled particle, information could be conveyed instantaneously to the other, regardless of the distance between. This concept was used in Quantum cryptography, sending extremely fast complicated codes, impossible to decode without the "key," to the entangled particles. Quantum computing allowed the computer to work at light speed instead of a relatively slow flow of electrons through circuits within a hard drive.

In theory, separating large quantities of entangled particles and creating two separate communication devices, like walkie-talkies, with these particles, made instantaneous communication possible across large distances, even across the far recesses of the universe.

It took eight minutes for sunlight to travel from the sun to the Earth. If the Sun were to implode and had one entangled walkie-talkie device by it when it did, then people on earth could find out the sun was gone eight minutes before they actually noticed, visually, that the sun was gone. This assumes the transmitting device from the sun was not destroyed of course. But what the heck would people really do with the knowledge they only had eight minutes of sunlight left? Still, the applications and advantages for deep-space travel were obvious.

In the beginning, Burton was focused on cryptography but had moved on to a more theoretical study of instantaneous communication. To prove his theory of instantaneous communication, he used his computer to communicate with a device that had been accelerated and was therefore in a different temporal reference frame.

This acceleration technique had already been tested through experiments using two cesium clocks. One clock was left on the Earth while another was flown around the planet in an airplane. The clock circling the earth, being accelerated in an airplane, actually lost time, and became younger than the clock that stayed on Earth. Even stranger was the proof that acceleration and gravity were equivalent. If acceleration made something younger then gravity too, which is caused by mass, made something younger as well. This is known as the 'Twin Paradox'. If twins were separated and one was placed on the top of a mountain, further away from the Earth's gravitational mass, and the other lived on the flatlands; the one on the mountain aged slower than the one on the flatland.

Burton's experimentation was to prove communication was possible with the past and future since the accelerated device would actually be a second or two behind that of the computer. So in his own little way, his instantaneous communication may in fact be with the future, albeit only seconds ahead. Eventually the plan was to be able to communicate with the future and the past using the quantum entangled devices. Knowing today what would happen tomorrow, would give the United States government a tremendous advantage. The United States could be the rulers of the world, and even, the universe. A single man, buried far beneath the earth, would have unveiled one large secret of God's code, and that would be Dr. Burton Carrier. Not that Burton had an ego, which he did, but this would change everything. He would be the conduit for the new hierarchy and potentially could define his own fate by knowing the future. Internally these visions of grandeur and dictatorship escaped the sensors of the polygraph, because, these were deep impressions, which were burned in his very soul. These were not dreams or aspirations; they were tied to his very being, as much as his blood and his mind.

As Burton approached the first door to the SCIF, Special Compartment Intelligence Facility, he thought, 'Today will be the day we actually communicate with the device in a different temporal plane. The future is now, the past will be tomorrow.'

Burton placed his chin on the shelf below the retina scan device and waited for the scan to complete. It verified his identity and allowed the heavy steel door to his office to be opened. The door latch popped with a loud 'clap'. He turned the handle and entered the 'the Man-Trap'; the space between two steel doors where he would have to use his badge and cipher code to proceed or be locked in until security arrived. He passed his badge in front of another scanner and typed in his cipher 35711. The door sprung open inward to the lab.

The sterile white-tiled floor combined with the brightly lit white ceilings and walls blinded the eyes. Inside the room, stood two stoic men wearing white lab coats almost camouflaged against the pristine whiteness. Their names were John Nelson and Harold Bottomly, and they were both Ph.D.s, extremely capable and eager to assist.

"Dr. Carrier, we are ready."

Burton nodded nonchalantly and took his seat at the computer console. He was in command. This was his universe. He knew the physics, he knew the computers, and soon he would know the future.

"I know." He responded curtly as if to say, "*Of course you are, you minions, and what should I expect from a couple of grads from MIT, incompetence?*"

"You have completed the test preparedness sequence?"

"Yes," they replied. "It's on the board."

He glanced at the white board and saw the times and tasks listed.

4:00 – 4:47 a.m.	Completed Computer Device 1 to Device 2 entangled particle confirmation test.
4:48 – 5:03 a.m.	Placed Device 2 in accelerator device. Closed the container surrounding Device 2, bolted closed using defined torque.
5:05 – 8:05 a.m.	Accelerated Device 2 to 1000 meters per second.
8:05 a.m.	Shut off Accelerator.
8:08 a.m.	Removed bolts from Device 2 container and removed Device 2 from Accelerator.
8:10 a.m.	Connected Device 2 to monitor in Closed room.

All seemed well. Device 2 now sat in another room approximately ten feet from Device 1, which was the computer where Burton was preparing his test code.

"Assuming we all know our physics, Device 2 is now thirty seconds younger than Device 1?"

"Correct Dr. Carrier."

"If I were to transmit an instantaneous quantum-entangled message from Device 1 to Device 2, I would not see it on Device 2 for thirty seconds, although we know the message is instantaneous. Correct?"

Burton's talking out loud allowed him to re-work and re-emphasize the complicated time-frame reference in his mind.

"Correct Dr. Carrier."

"Let's begin!"

Burton began typing on the computer: The Past is Today.

The lab assistants stared at the screen on the monitor connected to Device 2.

"Ready," they responded.

"Here we go," replied Burton as he hit the 'Send' button.

Immediately the two lab assistants yelled, "Damn it! NO!"

The message should have taken half a minute to appear on their screen. It was immediate. Burton closed his eyes and leaned his head backward.

"Why?" he asked softly, "Why?"

The three non-time travelers were silent for almost a minute.

Burton put his face into his hands and paused. He felt the weight of the universe on his shoulders. How could there be an error? He'd gone over everything numerous times. Whatever that error might be, he truly had no idea.

"That's enough for today," he said speaking through his hands, "I have to lie down and think. I don't know why it failed. By my calculations this should have worked!" Burton was disappointed, stumped and pissed. The disappointment was heard in his voice. "I need to rest."

It was quiet for a moment. The minions were frightened. They stared at him and wondered whether he *ever* rested. The mind of Dr. Carrier was in perpetual motion with constantly firing neurons. There was never any rest.

"Leave me alone!" he yelled. "Get out of here!" he said with anger. His people skills were lacking and seemed to totally disappear when he was frustrated and facing failure.

He spoke the words in his own mind.

'Tomorrow is another day . . . I expected to be there today.'

Chapter 6

> *The number of books will grow continually, and one can predict that a time will come when it will be almost as difficult to learn anything from books as from the direct study of the whole universe. It will be almost as convenient to search for some bit of truth concealed in nature as it will be to find it hidden away in an immense multitude of bound volumes.*
>
> *Denis Diderot*

Nicholas lived at the fabled Houdini Estate in Laurel Canyon, a favorite wooded haven from the hustle and bustle of Hollywood, home to many famous actors, writers, entertainers and artists. While Harry Houdini never actually lived on the property, he had spent time at the mansion and during the '30's Bess Houdini, his beloved wife, held parties and séances there in an attempt to communicate with her deceased husband. Nicholas' parents had purchased the property in 1958 after it had burned to the ground and built a rather large estate where Nicholas now lived. He oftentimes would walk the 3.5 acres that housed caves, fountains and a natural spring to feel nearer to his mother and father and to the world's greatest escape artist, Houdini.

But it was in Nicolas' library, whose arched windows overlooked the estate, where all of his true friends lived these days, post Amy. To him, his books were living entities, willing to share their deepest thoughts with an open mind. Reading provided the lessons of magicians, physicists, and martial artists who were long gone but lived on within the pages of the books. Nicholas was a collector of books, of fine first editions in a plethora of topics. His custom shelves, adorned with crown molding and sculpted facades, took over two years for him to build. It was a library he was proud of, both aesthetically and in content.

The library had one main circular room two stories high with a metal spiral staircase to a second floor and contained selections from Homer to Stephen King. A great archway on the west side of the rotunda enticed the reader to the entrance of the library. The rotunda itself was crowned with a huge stained glass dome depicting a wizard reminiscent of Gandalf. The bottom floor had three alcoves; each packed with books on a single subject. The alcove to the north was full of books on physics. Among them was a James Maxwell first edition on electrodynamics as well as a third edition of Newton's Principia di Mathematica. The alcove to the south contained books on Martial arts, philosophy, Semiotics, and Zen. The eastern alcove, where Nicholas was presently sitting, had shelves over-flowing with books on the practice and history of magic, sleight-of-hand, prestidigitation, and the annals of conjuring. He possessed some of the rarest books in print, including first editions of *Hocus Pocus Junior*, *The Anatomie of Legerdemain* from 1634, as well as Reginold Scot's *The Discoverie of Witchcraft* from 1584. He even had a first edition of Francis Bacon's *Sylva Sylvarum*, which described in considerable detail, a conjurer's use of a psychological force in the discovery of the identity of a selected object, and Bacon's analysis of the methods employed.

Tonight, the shelves were in a bit of disarray because he had been researching historical significance and methods of presentation for a new conjuring performance he had been working on.

A blazing fire crackled as Nicholas sat in a chair at his mahogany desk. He had decided to take a break from grading his students' final exams and had picked up a book on 'Magic and Meaning' by one of his idols, Eugene Burger, the sage of modern magic, when his phone rang.

"Hello?"

"Nicholas, this is Dean Roberts. I hope I haven't caught you at a bad time?"

"No, Dean Roberts. I was taking a break from the grading monotony anyway. What's up?"

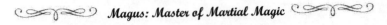

"I was wondering... could you possibly come to see me in my office before your 2 p.m. class tomorrow?"

"Sure – but what's up?" replied Nicholas.

"We'll discuss it tomorrow. See you then, thanks," and the Dean was gone, leaving Nicholas holding a dead phone, puzzled.

*   *   *

The university campus was a beautiful mixture of red brick academic buildings intermingled with sprawling lawns and large canopied trees. With one hundred seventy-four buildings on over four hundred acres, the school was one of the most sought-after universities to attend, and a most prestigious place to hold a teaching position.

The following afternoon, avoiding students on their way to class, Nicholas meandered through the campus grounds. He approached a three-story brick building and nearly collided with a vivacious co-ed exiting from the large glass doorway. Nicholas apologized and entered the building, walked down the hallway and knocked on the office door with a plaque that read: Dean Allan Roberts.

"Come in," said the familiar voice. Allan Roberts was a very distinguished-looking man, perfectly typecast as an elderly Dean of Science.

"Ah, Nicholas, glad you could come." Allan put down the book he was reading. The office held an eclectic collection of papers, books, diplomas, certificates and a scattering of children's artwork. His desk was cluttered in an academic display of submitted scientific periodical work, correspondence and yellow notebooks covered with illegible scribbles.

Allan motioned for Nicholas to sit, but he chose not to. He stood at the edge of Allan's desk.

"Please sit." And Allan motioned to the seat in front of the desk again.

"No thanks. I need to get to my class," Nicholas said, with a slight edge to his voice. "What's up?"

"Well, this is rather uncomfortable for me to say, but we have a problem."

"A problem?"

"Yes ... ah ... it appears that your magical endeavors are creating negative impressions with some of our major financial contributors."

"I'm sorry Dean Roberts, but what the hell are you talking about? You know I've never established an association between the University and any of my performances or extra-curricular activities."

"I know, Nick. I know. However, there is at least one very influential benefactor who is rather uncomfortable with the astrophysicist whose night job is that of a showman at local clubs. You're not yet Richard Feynman, and I know you are hoping for tenure. I was hoping we could discuss options for changing the opinions of the Board of Trustees. This gentleman seems to have a lot of influence at the University."

"I'm sorry; I didn't know that the University had control of my personal life, especially since it is not impacting my physics classes in any way..." Nicholas turned away from Dean Roberts, trying to mask his anger. He gazed out the window.

"Look, I know you were hoping for tenure. The vote, by the way, was unanimous not to grant you with tenure this year. They have a perception of how a scientist should behave and it doesn't include performing magic."

Nicholas was angry, but he calmed his mood and turned back to face the Dean, "I am very disappointed. You know my classes are some of the most popular classes at the school, and..."

Dean Roberts interrupted him, "I know Nick, but it is the perception that seems to be the problem. Your image isn't that of a scientist and a professor, but that of a nighttime carnie. Nick, these impressions are very important to the University. It reflects back on them. They have asked me to ask you to stop with the magic. Or if you have to, take some time off and perform full-time to get this out of your system and decide what it is you really want to be; an astrophysicist or a magician."

"That's not fair, Allan. I'm a well-respected scientist, magician and martial artist; a student of many things, a master of three."

"Nick, I am telling you the way it is. Something has to give." Allan paused.

Nicholas' mind raced in many directions. He realized anger should not be the determinant in his decision. Neither would spite, nor revenge, solve the problem. This was ridiculous. Maybe he should take a year off and just perform. Maybe he should take a sabbatical and go to the mountains with the strange monk. Now there was a crazy thought...

"You know what Dean? Maybe they're right. Maybe you've got the solution ... I'll take some time off; a sabbatical."

"Really? You would want to do that?" asked the Dean, surprised at the quickness of Nicholas' decision but disappointed at his choice.

"It doesn't seem like I have much of a choice. Recently I was asked by a Pakistani theologian to become a road scholar at his institution." Not entirely a lie. "I was considering it, and this just became the perfect time."

"Are you sure? ... I mean, you shouldn't rush into these things. Maybe the Board would..."

"No." Nicholas cut him off, "I am sure." He felt the weight lifting. He reached for the doorknob signaling that the meeting was about to end.

"I will prepare the appropriate paperwork tomorrow and take a year sabbatical. Don't worry. I will finish grading for this quarter. And thank you..."

"Ah... you're welcome... I guess."

"I assure you, I won't be the same character your Board and benefactors are worried about when I return. I can guarantee you that."

Chapter 7

> *Wasn't the water, the very essence of Martial Arts? I struck it, but it did not suffer. Again I stabbed at it with all my might, yet it was not wounded. I tried to grasp a handful of it, but it was impossible. This water, the softest substance in the world, could fit itself into any container. Although it seemed weak, it could penetrate the hardest substance. I wanted to be like the nature of water.*
>
> *Bruce Lee*

The Pacific Ocean in the Los Angeles basin never warmed up enough for the average swimmer to enjoy a prolonged swim off the coast without the protection of a wetsuit. Paradoxically, a swimmer wearing a wetsuit appeared seal-like, which was the standard food staple of the White Shark. In spite of the danger, there were still, of course, surfers who braved the Pacific, especially in the summer, looking for that ultimate wave, and the thrill ride of the century. The danger to them was worth the risk.

On this day, there was no heat wave and the beaches were deserted. A rare chilly spring storm had encroached on the Los Angeles coastline, turning the mostly blue skies to a color of dark gray. Low clouds moved in non-jet-stream directions as the low pressure in the atmosphere caused a swirl in the air currents. The skyline blended without a line of deviation with the darker gray ocean beneath. Occasional white caps defined the waves emanating from this fusion at the horizon.

Rain formed dimples on the surface of the sea. Amidst the turbulence of the waves, two bodies were visible intermittently through the veil of the gray ocean. Their heads burst through the water and their black bodies rose chest high. They wore wetsuits and goggles and were treading water about one hundred yards from the terra firma security of the shore.

They were Nicholas and his sister, Jen, performing their daily martial arts training in the water, using the ocean as their dojo. The resistance of the water heightened their movements into isometric muscle-strengthening exercises. The underwater movement of their punches and kicks affected not only each other, but provided a molecular domino effect of water all across the ocean. Their underwater training, in its own way, effected the entire environment under the Pacific Ocean.

They gasped for breath and treaded water as Jen spoke through the pelting of raindrops, "I don't understand."

Nicholas replied, "I have no choice. With the faculty Board refusing me tenure and the quarter over in a week, the timing is perfect. I don't want to become resentful of these benefactors, but if I stay, I will do just that. I need to get away, and who knows, maybe this will lead to some new research, some new ideas, and some new work to publish!"

Jen didn't acknowledge his answer.

"And I repeat, you're going where? You're going to study what? Are you insane?"

"I am going to study the ways of the Magi in a remote region between Pakistan and Tibet."

Jen looked incredulous.

"A guy does a card trick and you decide to follow him to Istanbul and join a religious cult to walk in the footsteps of Yoda? You don't even know this man."

"I know it sounds crazy, but what I saw was not a trick. I felt it and I knew it. He has an ability I want to learn. And there is something else... If I can learn what he can do, I will be even more than I am today, and I don't just mean as a magician or as an astrophysicist. There is something more; even in the brief time I spent with him in my dressing room, I feel in my deepest spirit, I will change."

He paused, trying to establish a sense of validity. "There's a reason I've been chosen to pursue this path. And there's a reason this is happening now."

Quickly he raised his arm, looked at his watch and said firmly, "Hajime!" That was the Japanese word for 'begin' and as the word was spoken, they slipped their goggles over their eyes, filled their lungs full of air and submerged below the gray waves of the sea.

Under the surface, there was silence. Nicholas and Jen pushed themselves down about ten feet below the surface and began performing Tai Chi-like moves in a slow fluid motion. These moves though, unlike Tai Chi, included kicks, punches and blocks. Jen sparred with her brother, blocking his thrusts. Their moves were once again beautifully choreographed as they performed a martial arts battle beneath the turbulent, stormy sea.

It was murky underwater, even more so than usual due to the stormy turbulence above the sea. Their visibility was limited to only about fifteen feet and towards the west was a kelp forest that completely blocked their view beyond ten feet towards the open sea.

They were both intensely focused on their training but both had an acute proximity sense under the sea as fish swam and scurried from their battle.

Peripherally they both sensed the shark immediately as it emerged from the kelp forest opening its jaw as it swam towards Jen. In the second they had to understand the situation Jen reached into her belt and removed her SpecWar diving knife from its sheath. Nicholas on the other hand turned his head towards the shark, and cocked his left hand by his hip for a punch. In an instant, the shark was upon them and Nicholas threw a very quick direct punch to the left gill of the shark as Jen stabbed her knife into the right eye of the predator. The shark snapped its mouth closed as it swam by them, swinging its head in pain. It continued beyond them into the depths flailing its head in both directions and sinking in depth. It disappeared into the dark void below.

Nicholas and Jen pushed up to the surface, gasping for air in the falling rain.

"Are you okay?" Nicholas yelled to Jen as they rose out of the water breathing heavily.

"Yes, I am fine," she said hesitantly.

Nicholas consciously slowed his breathing and began to release the tension in his muscles, "Well that is the second great white we have encountered this year. Perhaps they are moving their feeding grounds due to the change in water temperature."

Jen replied sarcastically, "Or perhaps you are signaling them mentally so as to enhance our training."

Nicholas smiled, "Well regardless, I am a bit disappointed you decided to stab instead of punch. You know the shark's snout and gills are its most vulnerable. There was no need to stab it. There is enough killing in the world as you well know Jen, and we do not need to be a part of it."

"I know, I panicked. I am a little off my mark, and not as focused, as I listen to you talk of this silly trip abroad!"

"I understand Jen, but I am hoping that by acquiring this radical kind of knowledge this summer, that I can actually discover some new principles for magic and even potentially, in physics. And hey, you never know, maybe even some mind-control over Great White Sharks."

"Yeah, right. And I'm sorry, but you mean by learning more *what* this summer?" She continued, "You mean more Zen Yogi from Dr. Mogogo?" She quieted down but continued more serious, "You know there's a war going on in Pakistan by the way? And you do remember terrorists, right? They're not very friendly to Americans. Or are you too busy doing magic, science, and martial arts to remember the reality of war? Do you really know 'what' you are getting yourself into and 'what' you are going to learn?"

Nicholas responded with vigor, "Of course I know the dangers of war. I am quite aware of the reality of terrorists. I also know that Mom and Dad never feared to go where they needed to go, regardless of the danger. Their photographs show that reality in a light no one else has ever captured. And look at us, taking on a great white shark without even batting an eye while sparring underwater." He reached and took his sister's hand in the water.

"Jen, there is a reason I must go. It is something deep inside telling me if I do not do this, I, and perhaps others, will deeply regret it. Mom and Dad always said we must follow our hearts. Amy always encouraged me in that, too."

Jen's throat tightened up at this reference and then she responded, "Yes, but following your heart doesn't mean leaving your brain behind! You are becoming more and more distant. Ever since Mom and Dad and Amy died, you've been aloof. You haven't dated, you don't seem to be interested in anything but martial arts and magic."

Nick closed his eyes, drew a slow breath, and in a deeply pained voice, replied, "There's not a day goes by that I don't think of Amy. I still ache from losing her. Why should I date when I know that no other woman would match up? It's not worth it." He paused and then continued in a stronger voice, "There's a reason why Mom and Dad were so creative and such superb photographers, and there's a reason why they encouraged us to pursue our dreams."

"And is there a reason they all died?" Jen blurted out. "There was no reason, no purpose. Their bodies were never found in the wreckage. For all we know, that mountain in the Andes could be where they are still fighting for their very survival. I mean, what's the deal? If you want to go somewhere, let's go back to the site of their plane crash and start the search all over again. I mean it, Nicholas, where are they? Where for God's sake are they?"

"Jen, I don't know," he said quietly. "You and I both know, they could never have survived that crash, and if they had, they would have contacted us by now. That was three years ago. They were in an extremely remote area, and no one, us included, ever found any sign of their survival."

"Or of their death," responded Jen quickly.

Nicholas looked at his watch, "Okay, okay ... We can't keep re-hashing this. We are not progressing towards the truth. It's the truth that we should be searching for. I can learn something from any experience, whatever the outcome may be. So, I have decided to go to Pakistan."

"I've lost Mom and Dad... and I'm afraid of losing you, too."

"You won't lose me, Jen..." he looked at her appreciatively. He grabbed her and hugged her tightly, the two of them treading water with only their feet.

"But have you forgotten, you have an internship in D.C. this summer... I'm actually the one losing you."

He looked at his watch, "But for now, we are late, Hajime!"

Nicholas and Jen submerged into the sea with a splash. The circular waves expanded away from their points of departure from the surface.

Chapter 8

Many of life's failures are people who did not realize how close they were to success when they gave up.

Thomas A. Edison

Burton Carrier lay on his cot-like bed, legs crossed, staring at the ceiling, with his hands behind his head. His hair had that wind-swept look, even though he hadn't been in a wind, much less a breeze, in months. His frustration at the failed experiment had thrown him. Failure wasn't in his plan. This was supposed to be the crowning moment of success when his hypothesis was proven correct.

His room in the underground abode was similar to what might be found on a submarine, although bigger and a lot more comfortable. And he didn't have to share it with anyone. That was a very good thing. He had a single bed, a small kitchen area with microwave (for accelerating particles of a different kind), a bathroom, and a work area with the requisite desk and computer. For such small quarters, the place was immaculate. His obsessive-compulsive behavior was in full evidence here. Everything was always exactly where it needed to be, folded, and put away. Everything was perfect in the world under his control.

Or at least the physical world, but now, he needed to deal with the imperfection that was gouging at his mind, and the thoughts raced furiously, "Why didn't it work?"

He turned over on his side and curled into a fetal position, keeping his hands on his head as if trying to stop the thoughts that were racing through his mind. He began to rock back and forth: 'Why didn't it work? It should have, everything went by the book… It was easy… Of course if it was that easy, anyone could do it…

Everything was as it should have been, and yet, we failed. I failed. Perhaps it has to do with the method of observation?'

'But I know I can do it. So why didn't it work? What am I missing? What am I not seeing?' He rocked back and forth, salving his soul. Then...

'That's it...' he bolted up from his prone position. 'Observation...' he pondered. Quantum physics was a quandary of logical puzzles, many of which were based on just how things were being observed, when they were observed, and even if they were observed.

"Both devices were being observed," he said out loud. "That's what I wasn't seeing!!"

He then said it louder with more conviction, "Both particles were being observed!"

"That's it!" he yelled. "They were both observed at the same time, in the same time, in the same temporal reference frame, thus collapsing the ethereal wave functions into the present, negating the accelerated reference frame." He thought, 'So, the problem really stems from the fact that both devices were constantly being observed. If the device that was accelerated was not being observed when it was being communicated with, even for a nanosecond, this would allow it to become the device of the past. It was the act of observation which forced the experiment not to work.'

"Hmmmmm."

'So,' he thought, 'I must try again, and not observe the accelerated device, but take data while I communicate with it, then the wave function might just be stable in the future state.'

He considered this approach and found it logically sound.

He hopped out of bed and called his minions in the lab. He asked them to perform the set-up as they had previously and then to leave the lab for the evening.

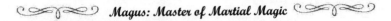

'Go home,' he thought, 'and play with your families, while I play God.'

*   *   *

Burton entered the lab at around 11:45 p.m. that evening.

He checked the white board.

Everything was in order.

The entangled device in the other room had been accelerated. There was no one there to observe the message that he would type and send from his own screen. The message would be sent, and the computer would time-stamp the arrival of the message on the far screen. He would check its arrival later.

He sat at the terminal of entangled device one, and typed his message: *The future is tonight.*

He sat for a moment to think through the set-up and confirm in his mind that all was as it should be.

He hit 'send' and waited.

At about the ten-second mark, a message came across the display at Device 1 in response: *However, the past is what will determine your future.*

Burton excitedly jumped up and ran to the window in the room where Device 2 sat idle. Not as idle as he had thought. Immediately, he saw that the display revealed his original words, *The future is tonight.* However, there was no one in the other room; there was no one who could have typed the response. There were no other connections. This made absolutely no sense.

Back at Device 1 he typed his inquiry: *Is someone else connected to this network?* and he hit 'send'.

He waited.

Yes, appeared on his screen.

He typed: *Who are you?*

How the hell could there be anyone else connected to his devices? Talk about secure. He was miles beneath the surface locked away in a SCIF office within lead walls, with only two devices that shared the same entangled particles.

His display lit up with a response: *More importantly, where and when are you?*

'Shit!' he thought. 'This is way beyond me. Where and when??? I don't get it. Have I breached security? Is there a spy in my department? And more importantly, what if someone else is ahead of me in this experiment?'

His display lit up again: *I see we have a predicament. Neither of us knows whom we are talking to, and you are not prepared to reveal your situation. Are we correct?*

Burton looked at the message, considered the proverbial "we" aspect. At a loss of what to do, Burton stared at the screen.

The screen responded to the ether: *Are you alone?*

'Yes,' Burton thought. 'I am alone and right now wishing the hell I wasn't.' He continued looking at the screen, hoping something would make sense. He thought to himself, 'What harm would a response to this question cause? No security breach as far as I can tell.' He typed: *Yes*.

There was silence. It lasted for at least a minute, and then his display lit up with the response: *Good. We have much to talk about. At the very least, we must make the assumption you are on Earth. Where we are for the moment is unimportant. We must also assume you are the first to use this type of device, because yours is the first message we have received. We must congratulate you on your success! You are a very special being in the plan of the cosmos. You will have a special place in the annals of existence, and will be a king amongst the populace.*

Burton looked at the screen and liked what he saw. But still, who could this be? He needed more information. He needed to pry, because he needed to know.

He typed: *I very much appreciate the praise, and my success is indeed sweet, but it has lost some of its grandeur due to your participation. I must know who you are!*

His display responded: *Who is important. Where is important. However, for now let us start with "When" for the response. I suspect that you are approximately fifty thousand years in our future based on our interpretation of the current temporal settings within your computer.*

Chapter 9

*Every rock seems to glow with life. Some lean
back in majestic repose; others, absolutely
sheer, or nearly so, for thousands of feet,
advance their brows in thoughtful attitudes
beyond their companions, and the winds shine
and surge and wreathe about them as the years
go by, as if into these mountain mansions
Nature had taken pains to gather her choicest
treasures to draw her lovers into close and
confiding communion with her.*

John Muir

A Pakistani International Airlines C-130 aircraft, operated
by the Air Force, flew over one of the most scenic areas from
Islamabad to the Gilgit Airport: the Karakoram Mountain Range.
Karakoram, in Turkish, meant 'black gravel' as many of the glaciers
were covered in black fractured rocks. Nicholas was awed by the
aerial views of the rugged, natural beauty of these mountains. The
snow-covered peaks and pristine blue lakes nestled at the foot of the
mountains hid the rough terrain, sharp angled slopes and climate
extremes. He knew his hiking abilities were about to be challenged.

The Karakoram mountain range was like no other. It
possessed the loftiest peaks in the world, all within a radius of one
hundred miles of a single point. There were over eighty-two peaks
exceeding twenty-three thousand feet in height. Many of these
peaks were untouched, unclimbed and un-named. The Karakorams
differed from other mountains due to their angular, sharp, icy
peaks, often surrounded by incredible clusters of towers and spires,
piercing through the clouds into the heavens. There were fewer
monsoons here than in the Himalayas, and in fact, many of the deep
valleys were lush with vegetation. These valleys were hidden
beneath the monolithic grandeur of the mountains and were haven
to many a creature, some yet to be discovered. The Karakorams and

the Himalayas were two of the world's most geologically active areas, at the boundary between two colliding continents and were important to Earth scientists in the study of plate tectonics.

Ahura and Nicholas de-planed in Gilgit, the capital city of Northern Pakistan. The terrain around Gilgit was very mountainous; an ancient trading post, whose bustling bazaar offered wares from China and India for many of the traders of the Silk Road. Its dusty, old-world ambience was largely unaffected by the travelers and the potpourri of people that occupied and visited it. Lush green terraced gardens; orchards of apricots, cherries and apples were interspersed throughout the town.

It wasn't long before Ahura had acquired two yaks and supplies for their trek up the mountain. The Yak, a mountain dweller's beast of burden, looked like a shaggy and fierce-looking cow, but was extremely docile. On the sides of the hills, shepherds and their sheep watched as the two men guided their yaks in the rain along the cart path. The yaks were stacked to the hilt with supplies for their journey into the mountains. Nicholas knew this was no ordinary journey and these were no ordinary mountains.

The gentle rain continued as the two travelers walked slowly beside their beasts of burden.

As the rain picked up, Nicholas turned to Ahura and said, "And I left sunny Southern California for this? I've never been so cold!" He waved his hand towards the rain and the sky.

"Yes, and I came back for this," responded Ahura. He gestured with his hand to the picturesque mountains, "Up above, no rain. Up there, it snows. But you can never see in California what you see here."

They continued in silence until Ahura proceeded with his geography lesson, "Of course, there are many valleys that are very lush, and very pretty. You will see soon enough."

"How soon?" inquired Nicholas.

"We will walk for six days," responded Ahura.

"Six days..." Nicholas repeated softly. He sighed as they continued. His expectations were not a trek in mud and snow into a mountainous region for six days. He wanted to learn magic. Real Magic; the kind of magic he saw Ahura produce in his dressing room.

The rain began to let up. Off to the side of the cart path, on the hillside, people looked up from their fieldwork to stare at the travelers.

Nicholas looked towards them as he said, "They look scared."

Ahura shook his head and said, "Do you really think they look scared? Really?" He was looking for the truth, not idle conversation.

Nicholas responded, obviously caught in his attempt to make conversation.

"Okay, maybe not scared, perhaps curious."

"Perhaps," said Ahura. "But what do you really think they feel? Or, are you only making conversation?"

"Okay..." Nicholas said, and then paused and looked at the people in the fields and they looked back.

"They seem curious, but also seem to know we are going into the mountains, umm, for a reason. They think it is beyond them, but they accept it. They are curious to see us pass, but they think they know where we are going and even think they know our journey will be long and arduous."

Ahura smiled and said, "Very good. This empathetic display is your first taste of understanding your relationship to the environment around you; observation without judgment. Yes, it is only a beginning, but we will feed this ability and you will progress." His emphasis was on the word "will."

"In addition," he continued, "I think we should start the repetitions now."

"The what?" inquired Nicholas.

Ahura responded nonchalantly, "The repetitions." He paused while Nicholas still looked puzzled.

"This exercise will develop your empathetic talents, your first step on the path to real understanding and true magic."

Nicholas listened, still not understanding, as Ahura continued, "True magic demands the understanding of relationships that exist between everything, animate and inanimate. The first step in understanding is sensing the world around you; to improve your already inherent empathetic talents of being able to sense what others are feeling. Eventually you will be able to control these feelings and thereby control the reality of the emotional environment around you."

"I have a rather fine understanding of the relationships between matter in the material world," stated Nicholas confidently.

"Yes, but I am not talking about physics but instead, emotional connectivity. By learning how to observe by listening, you will begin to understand the feelings of others. Let's start. By the time we get to our destination you will have learned at the very least, what you need to enter the Magi Cloister, although you may also wish you had taken a vow of silence instead."

"I have a choice?" responded Nicholas.

"You always have a choice. There are many paths in life and death, and there are many options. Who is to say whether or not all these options are or are not being fulfilled in a different reality?" answered Ahura.

"I know I have choices in life, I was referring to the Cloister," responded Nicholas sarcastically. "Do they speak in the Cloister, or have they all taken a vow of silence?"

Ahura began, "Enough of that. You will see soon enough. Now, repeat after me with an honest answer. For example, if I say 'You have a green shirt,' you say, 'I have a green shirt,' since you do. If you do not have green shirt and I say you do, feel free to answer with, 'I do not have a green shirt,' or 'No, I have a blue shirt.' And then I will repeat what you say, honestly and then you repeat that and so on. Okay?"

"Okay?" repeated Nicholas trying to be funny. Ahura, aware of this humorous attempt, smiled and continued, "You will understand more as we go."

"The anticipation is killing me," said Nicholas.

"You have a green shirt," said Ahura.

"I have a green shirt," said Nicholas somewhat non-committal.

"You have a green shirt," responded Ahura with the same lack of commitment as Nicholas.

Nicholas responded quicker, "I have a green shirt."

Ahura kept up the pace, "You have a green shirt."

Quicker still Nicholas responded, "I have a green shirt."

"You have a green shirt," responded Ahura maintaining exact speed and inflection.

"I have a green shirt," said Nicholas.

"You have a green shirt," said Ahura.

"I have a green shirt," said Nicholas with a bit of irritation in his voice.

"You have a green shirt," responded Ahura with the same inflection of irritation and frustration as Nicholas.

"Yes, I have a green shirt!" responded Nicholas getting angrier still.

"Yes, you have a green shirt!" answered Ahura in a mocking tone.

"Yes! Damn it! I have a green shirt!" responded Nicholas with real anger.

"Yes! Damn it! You have a green shirt!" said Ahura continuing to mock the anger.

"Okay!" said Nicholas still angry.

"Okay!" said Ahura getting a little quieter.

"Okay!"

"Okay."

"Okay," said Nicholas beginning to submit to the exercise.

"Okay."

"Okay."

Silence. The yaks trotted on ignorant of their exercise, the anger, the lull, and even the potential empathetic growth, which may have occurred. Ahura focused on the mountains in silence and Nicholas followed his gaze as his adrenaline returned to normal. He took a deep breath.

Ahura spoke as he stared at the pinnacles, "What a truly enlightening discourse."

Nicholas removed his eyes from the mountains and stared at Ahura, evaluating his sanity.

Ahura continued, "I am sure you felt it, regardless of the apparent confusion you now feel. By truly listening, you can learn to observe and to feel what is happening inside others and in the aura around them. This is our goal: To truly listen and to be aware of what is happening around us." He paused as Nicholas continued to stare in bewilderment. "Let us start again."

Nicholas quickly awakened from his daze, "NO! PLEASE!" he said in a tone not unlike a homeless beggar.

The "NO PLEASE" repetitions echoed off the slopes and diminished as the two men trekked up the beginnings of the trail into the Karakoram Range. The moon was rising in the "V" between two mountains and the sun had begun to slowly fade its glare behind them as they started their journey into a new realm.

Chapter 10

*The most beautiful experience we can have is
the mysterious.*

Albert Einstein

Dusk settled over the mountainous realm. There were hints of light between the huge monoliths. The sky was full of stars but only a select few were visible, unscreened by the mountains, at the zenith points above the magicians. The travelers who had camped in the valley ignored these few stellar entities. Ahura and Nicholas sat by the crackling fire and focused on the flames and the warmth radiating from the logs. Their bedrolls were spread close to the fire.

Nicholas stared into the flames but his thoughts drifted to his current situation. His mind pondered a plethora of questions and concerns. Perhaps his sister was correct. What was he doing here in the middle of nowhere traveling with a guru from an unknown monastery? Why wasn't he practicing on the beach in Southern California watching the waves of the summer Pacific tumble along the sand? As he contemplated, he grabbed a stick and poked at the fire causing sparks to pop and unfurl. He watched them rise into the night and laid back down on his bedroll.

Nicholas idly mused, and asked of Ahura or maybe the stars, "Did you know that until 1774 combustion was not really understood?"

He paused, not expecting an answer to the question. Ahura stared at the fire intently as Nicholas continued on a lengthy discourse.

"Many people believed fire was a basic element of the universe. There was fire, water, earth and air. That was it. Some experiments by a French chemist named Lavoisier gave us our present understanding of combustion. But even with our understanding of combustion, the complexity of what happens inside a candle flame is beyond us. There are several levels of complexity, the non-luminous inner portion where the wax produces gases..."

While Nicholas lectured, Ahura pondered the flames, oblivious to the conversation, or at the very least, he appeared not interested. He focused on the real fire, not the theory. He raised his hands in front of his body and began to make a motion as if he was pulling an invisible elastic band and letting it go. He continued this motion as the flames began to grow.

Nicholas stared at the sky ignorant of the growing flames, and continued, "And the middle zone where the gases are decomposed to hydrogen, which burns..."

The flames grew larger while Nicholas stared at the sky. Ahura's movements and focus were broader now. Nicholas was oblivious to the shaman-like magic Ahura was performing.

"... carbon heated to incandescence..."

A low rumble began to emit from the fire as the flames grew.

"... and finally, an outer, hardly visible region where combustion is complete, where carbon dioxide and water are formed. But although we understand the science, we don't understand..."

The rumbling noise from the fire became much louder. Nicholas sat up suddenly and saw the flames were much taller and more fierce than a normal fire would have produced.

"What the..."

Suddenly, the fire exploded into a huge ball of flame that rose from the pit up into the sky and the darkness above. It rose and diminished into a speck, resembling one of the stars as it joined the abundance of twinkling brethren amongst the cosmos.

Nicholas was speechless as he stared upward. There were more stars above them than he had ever seen in a small area of space framed on all sides by the black monolithic mountains. And he was amazed at the combustion that just occurred while he had been busy rambling on about the physics of fire. He remembered for a moment why he was truly on this journey.

Ahura spoke softly, as he continued to stare at the fire, "You need not know the chemical equations for the flame to know what it truly is, or to know its relationship to the rest of the universe, or how to control it."

Nicholas blinked and stared now at Ahura.

Ahura continued, "As a Magi Initiate you have much to learn. You are no longer the expert and you must start anew to walk down this path. Your knowledge may act either as a hindrance or an asset. Be careful how you use it. Focus on the lesson at hand."

There was a long silent pause punctuated by the crackling fire. The fire was re-establishing its control over the firmament.

Finally, Ahura spoke, "You have a green shirt."

Chapter 11

Nothing is easier than to denounce the evildoer; nothing is more difficult than to understand him.

Fyodor Dostoevsky

Burton stared at the computer. The lab was dark, except for the blue-white essence from the computer monitor, reflecting off his reading glasses. His vision was deteriorating faster than most. He thought it was due to all his years of staring at a computer screen.

The computer screen revealed dialogue, on the other hand, that was far-sighted as well as far-reaching:

It has been sometime since I have spoken to anyone, but I believe our conversation is representative of the time. There is movement amongst the Outsiders. I suspect they have found a new leader born of the realm. The universe has indeed changed since the time I am presently in. There have been, and are now, happenings beyond your knowledge of your world, which will soon be juxtaposed with your civilization. Paths will cross sooner than you know. Hopefully, the world will change sooner than the Outsiders are prepared for. The Coming will indeed occur. We would be very pleased if you would be our representative during these times of change and evolution.

'Representative.' Burton considered. 'What exactly does that mean?' He was still at a loss. Yes, this was all fascinating but he was a meat and potatoes kind of person. 'Where's the beef? What are we talking about here?' He needed facts. His calculating mind was not exactly filling the cosmos (or the room for that matter) with solutions.

We understand you need more information and I will be providing you that. But first, we must communicate in your present. I cannot tell you how things have evolved unless we speak directly in your current temporal plane. I will teach you how. We will need, however, to retain this quantum-connection still, to assist you and us with our final objective.

Dr. Carrier, you will need to work with us on your mental advancement. You must be extremely intelligent to have formulated a path for this communication, and we wish to assist you along a path of further mental development and power. You will have the power to change the world as you know it, and you will indeed be a leader in the world of the future. It will be a world full of opportunity to excel and to conquer.

But first, you must open your mind to the information we will be conveying to you. We can transfer all the programs you will need to take control of your leader's resources and power; but you must prepare your mind for the enemy and the future, because taking power from your government is only a stepping-stone in the path towards the real battle to come.

The door to the lab opened quickly and one of the minions, John, entered and flicked on the lights. A young, chubby, pimple-faced girl, wearing Goth-like apparel, accompanied him. She did not look like anyone who was capable of acquiring a security clearance, but of course, at first appearance she also did not look like anyone capable of being intelligent enough to sell secrets to foreign entities either.

Burton jumped and made a muffled "yelp" as he was startled at the loud 'pop' as the latch on the door clicked open after the lock had been released. He quickly shut down the system, and pushed his chair away from the computer.

"I'm sorry, Dr. Carrier. I didn't mean to startle you," John said sincerely. "I didn't think anyone was here. It was so dark."

Burton stared at him and the person he was with, "Yes, I needed some peace with my thoughts."

"Dr. Carrier..." He turned to the new intern. John pulled the girl forward.

"I would like to introduce you to Ursula Petrowski, our new intern. Dr. Carrier, Ursula. Ursula, Dr. Carrier."

Ursula reached out her hand. "Very pleased to meet you, Dr. Carrier."

"Likewise," Burton responded stoically. Absentmindedly, Burton turned to his office and walked away. Ursula withdrew her hand as John pushed her to follow him.

"I...I...I figured I'd give her a tour," John stammered.

"Not necessary," responded Burton. "We won't need an intern this summer. There must have been some miscommunication. I'm tired and will be going to my quarters." He rudely turned away from them and had an after thought, "And by the way, don't touch anything!" And with that, he was gone.

John apologetically looked to Ursula. "Sorry – he's a little eccentric and sometimes a bit rude. I thought he said he wanted an intern. My mistake. Sorry."

"I'd say he was a little rude. I wouldn't want to work for him anyway. And this looks like a very boring office! You did me a favor. I have some friends at a Crystal City facility anyway which is where I really wanted to work," she paused and looked around. "They actually have windows there."

Chapter 12

> *You'll wonder when I am coming.*
> *You'll wonder more when I am gone.*

Max Malini, the Magician of Kings

The sun shone brightly down on the travelers as they progressed up a remote, narrow trail along the side of the Karakoram mountain range. Rain slides had deposited rubble from above in several places along the trail that blocked the path or had washed it completely away. The going was grueling and treacherous. One could not lose focus.

One traveler spoke to the other, "You have a blue shirt."

The other responded calmly, "I have a blue shirt."

They repeated this back and forth, first one traveler, and then the other. Winding up the mountains, the trail hidden from the sun was dotted with small patches of snow and ice. The snow deepened as they ascended.

Nicholas felt a deep sense of wonder. The surroundings were breathtaking. This was an amazing experience but the repetitions were boring and lulling him to sleep. Yet with the path so dangerous, he had to fight to remain alert. What did the repetitions have to do with the magic? Ahura seemed nice enough, and wise enough, but the trek so far had been less magical than Nicholas would have hoped (although the fireball was rather impressive). Perhaps it was the altitude, perhaps it was the cold, but he wished he had not committed himself to this journey. He believed he knew what magic was, what science was about, and what the universe was capable of doing. He was loosing faith in his decision.

As these thoughts danced through his mind, the two travelers came upon the end of the trail. There was a rock and ice wall on their left, a snow-covered trail beneath them and a two thousand foot drop to their right. In front of them, a wall of twisted icicles blocked the path. They resembled misshapen bars that protected the external world from a troll, or more forebodingly, an abominable snowman. There was a cave, ten feet high, or at least, a large dark recess behind the icicles.

Ahura broke off some frozen spikes. Nicholas removed two stubborn, thick icicles with a Shotokan side-thrust kick. The yaks, happy to be stopping for a break, watched without concern. Their whiskers had frozen into small frosty icicles around their mouths. They shook their shaggy coats and shifted from hoof to hoof, in an effort to keep warm.

Ahura spoke calmly, "The six days have passed. It is time for me to leave you."

Nicholas looked at him in bewilderment.

"Excuse me! Leave me?"

Calmly Ahura continued, "I said I would bring you to the Magi. I did not say I would stay. I am only the guide, the vision to assist you along the path."

Nicholas began to lose his composure.

"You are going to leave me in this godforsaken mountain range to freeze my ass off?"

"No, I mean that I have brought you to the Cloister of the Magi and it is now your choice to proceed along the path... or not. God has definitely not forsaken this mountain range."

There was a moment of quiet on the path as Nicholas took his gaze from Ahura and looked inside the deep, dark cave. The wind blew through their clothes and hair; the cold was persistent.

"They are expecting you," said Ahura, very nonchalantly.

Nicholas turned his head back towards Ahura to begin another tirade of accusations, only to find Ahura gone. His anger toward Ahura turned to befuddlement and confusion. The two yaks were standing in the snow, perfectly oblivious to the loss of one of the travelers, looking comical with their frozen whiskers and iced shaggy coats.

"Ahura!" Nicholas called out, but he knew Ahura, wherever he was, could not hear him, nor would he respond if he could. Nicholas finally turned to the yaks and stamped his feet as he yelled, "SHIT!"

The word echoed through the valley below and a small avalanche of snow fell onto his head, a further exasperation. He looked rather silly. He kicked the snow, cursed under his breath, and tried to get as much snow from off his head and neck as he could. He was cold and alone. He mumbled to himself, "Great, now there are three yakasses in the snow."

He looked into the cave and turned back to the yaks. The snowfall began to pelt them harder as he said, "Alright, let's go."

He grabbed the yaks' reins and proceeded cautiously inside the cave. The sunlight lit up the entrance but soon he would need a flashlight. He grabbed a light from one of the saddlebags and turned it on, mumbling as he dragged the beasts of burden into the lightless void, "And to think I gave up crocheting by the fireplace for this."

The solitary flashlight beam lit the way as they progressed further into the cave. At least it was warmer inside, and there was no wind howling in his ears. Nicholas could hear water drops falling from the ceiling. The further they went into the cave the wetter it got.

Nicholas thought to himself, 'I'm getting soaked inside a cave! If I go back outside I'll freeze. What a choice...'

His light explored the sides of the walls and finally the wall in front of him. It was a dead end! His anger became subdued as he realized that the wall wasn't a wall at all, but a door! It was a large wooden door with black iron braces. It looked a thousand years old, splintered from age and worn from the harsh weather of the mountains. There was a large iron knocker at the height of Nicholas' head.

"I guess I should knock," he said, rather apprehensively.

Nicholas recapped his current situation in his mind: He was alone, with two yaks, in a cave a mile into a mountain in the middle of Northern Pakistan, hundreds of miles from civilization and he was knocking on an ancient door in the dark. Always a good thing to know where you stand.

He picked up the heavy knocker and banged twice against the wood. The sound resounded through the cavern and startled the yaks. Then there was only the sound of dripping water again, and from somewhere behind the door, the sound of footsteps.

Nicholas heard a muffled voice. It was English but was of an old, more poetic timbre. The voice sounded very proper and had a tone of authority.

"Who, may I ask, is requesting to cross the Threshold of the Infinite?"

Nicholas, hesitant and a little uncertain about how to respond, muttered, "Uh …Nicholas Thompson …I was told I'm expected."

The massive door slowly creaked open and a man's smiling face, complete with a full, albeit well trimmed, beard appeared around the edge of the door. He was backlit with flames from a torch.

"Well Nicholas, of course you are expected! I just wanted to inquire if you truly knew who you were."

Nicholas was getting a little annoyed again, "Of course I know who I am, but who are you?"

The bearded man responded, excited and happy regardless of Nicholas' apparent frustration, "Truthfully, I am not sure you know who you are, but I know who you are, and I think I know that you really do not know, exactly what you do not know, but I know I can help. Regardless, I am known as Rada Singh. My friends call me Rada."

Rada shoved the huge door open completely and extended his hand towards Nicholas, "I am very pleased to make your acquaintance."

Nicholas stared at the bearded man, dressed in an off-white robe with a hood draping behind him underneath his long hair. He looked to be in his early thirties; there was no grey yet, in his beard or hair. Nicholas thought he looked rather well groomed for a cave man. He had his hair pulled back in a ponytail behind his head and his beard appeared trimmed to a clean inch from his skin. And while his skin was well tanned, his heritage looked to be a blend of Caucasian, or more precisely Greek statue, and middle Eastern. He had neither blemish nor scar anywhere on his face, and his eyes were very white, with a deep green hazel hue.

Nicholas extended his hand and shook hands with Rada.

"Nice to meet you as well, I think, and as I said, my name is Nicholas Thompson, but my friends call me Nick."

Rada smiled as he pulled Nicholas and the yaks through the entrance.

"Well, welcome Dr. Nick to the Cloister of the Magi," said Rada with a hint of Wonder and Awe. He waved his free hand in an arc through the air revealing a huge chasm. "It is best we shelter you from the unfriendly world outside."

The cavern that Nicholas saw completely dumfounded him. He drew in a quick breath and held it, with his eyes open wide, as he tried to take in the massive void of the rock within the mountain. The cave was about half a mile deep and a thousand feet high. Torches at all levels provided light. There were hundreds of smaller cave entrances speckling the walls from the ground to the ceiling. It appeared that there were tunnels piercing through the ceiling. Wooden ladders, fastened to the walls led to the tunnel entrances from the floor of the main cavern. Each of the side caves had a torch on either side of its entrance. There were a few people dressed like

Rada climbing in and out of the caves, but for the most part the chasm was empty.

There was no sound. Nicholas felt a low vibration, like a hum going through his body. 'Unbound electrical current', he thought. He saw no signs of civilized light sources. The hum was all around him and within him. He could feel it, and he felt more aware than he had ever felt before in his whole life. It reminded him of a phenomenon known as the 'Taos Hum'. He had read about it on the web, but had dismissed it from his mind, until now.

He felt like he was part of the cave, part of the wall, part of the floor, part of the air, and even in harmony with his unusual guide, Rada. Although he should have been concerned and worried after what he'd been through, he was surprised that he felt no fear. He felt 'in the now'; he was where he needed to be, where he should be, and all was as it should be in the universe.

From the far end of the cavern, a bright light emitted a glow from a tunnel.

Nicholas stared all around him in awe. He was amazed; the cave was very impressive.

He said, "Not exactly what I was expecting."

"And if you do not mind my asking, what exactly were you expecting?"

"I'm not sure, but this isn't it!"

Rada answered, "Perhaps the absence of expectation is best. Most of us have never been outside the Cloister, at least not physically, so for us, this is our world, our home. This is the Old Wing of the Cloister, where the original Magi came to ponder the mysteries of the universe and to resolve the unknown. Our oldest Brethren still refer to it as the Labyrinth of the Infinite. The rest of us call it the Old Wing. The New Wing is through there," Rada pointed toward the light at the end of the cavern.

"In there, there are no mysteries, only opportunities of ambiguous precision."

Nicholas responded with some sarcasm. "Ambiguous precision... Thanks for the clarification."

It seemed that Rada was speaking English rather well for a man who had been confined to a monastery in the middle of the Pakistani mountains all his life. Either that, or 'ambiguous precision' was not an intentional oxymoron, but a mistake in his choice of words.

Rada seemed to understand the dilemma Nicholas was pondering, "I made no mistake in my description. I am fairly well versed in over fifty languages, and understand very well the meaning of each word I choose to speak."

They walked down the center of the cavern toward the far end. It was much warmer, a little too warm so Nicholas unzipped his tundra jacket. Rada guided the yaks as Nicholas looked around in awe at the caves in the walls and the shear magnitude of the cavern. Rada seemed to glide with the grace of a panther. Nicholas stopped and watched as an elderly man began a descent down one of the ladders from a cave very high above them.

Intrigued, Nicholas asked, "So, if this is the Old Wing, why are people still occupying the caves?" He pointed to the man on the ladder, "And what do you mean they've never physically left the Cloister? They've left mentally?"

Rada nodded in the affirmative and said, "But there is much more to it than that, and we will get to that soon enough when we meet with the Council."

"For now, let me tell you the caves in the Old Wing are a doorway to the Labyrinth of the Infinite as the old ones say, BUT you do not go into the labyrinth until you are ready. Trust me on this: Infinity is a big place, and many get lost."

Nicholas responded, making fun of Rada, but acknowledging his own lack of understanding.

"No problem there, Sahib, I don't plan on going anywhere without a guide or the Navy Seals. Truthfully, this place is a little scary and very much overwhelming... So you are saying that a bunch of magicians, or Magi, have been hiding out here, for how many years?"

"The Magi have been here for over two-thousand years, thanks to the travels of Pythagoras and others before him. Otherwise, we would not exist, at least not in your world. The council will give you an earthly history lesson later. You need not worry about that now. We need to get you settled in your chamber first. We are going to be in the same alcove which is truly an honor!"

"An honor for whom?"

"An honor for me, of course. You may not know who you are, but you will. True magic may one day return to your world in a big way. And I believe you will play a large part in its return."

Rada pulled the yaks away. Nicholas responded again with sarcasm under his breath, "Well, I must say though, I am bemused that I am the last to find out who I am. You'd think I would be one of the first to know, BUT NO, here I am following a couple of yaks around the Halls of Montezuma and I am going to be part of some huge magical revolution. I should be deserving of the honor of sharing your alcove, why not?" If Rada could or did hear Nicholas' ranting, he made no sign.

When they reached the far side, Nicholas realized the light coming into the cavern was not from an outside source, but rather from a bright luminosity emitting through cracks of a door to the outside. Light haloed around the great arched doorway indicative of even perhaps a great star beyond the wooden barrier. In the near darkness where they had been walking, any bright light would have seemed like the light of a super nova exploding above the earth.

Rada grabbed the door handle and said as he opened the door, "Here we are, the New Wing!"

He slowly pulled the heavy door open and again Nicholas' breath caught in his throat. As he moved through the doorway, he squinted and covered his eyes letting them slowly adjust to the new abundance of light. He had never seen anything so beautiful and wonderful as the snow-covered ridge projecting out and protecting a large rock-hewn village. The village was about twenty stories high, snuggled within this mountainous cavity. A colossal cone-shaped structure stood against the back wall of the cave, stairs ramping up to it from either side of the cavern in a semi-circular fashion along the walls. The cone had three very large windows near the top facing three compass directions.

The sun was shining brightly on this side of the tunnel they had just traversed. There was no longer a blizzard, but a clear blue sky. The air was still, crisp and fresh, no longer freezing, harsh, or windy.

People of all ages walked between the structures; most dressed in robes like Rada's, some blue, some black, and a few were an earthy green. Below the village, a valley stretched across several miles with lush green terraced gardens and fields in full bloom. A river ran through the center of the valley oasis, nestled with conifers and oaks along its banks, providing a spectacular scene.

People bowed to Rada and motioned in what appeared to be a salute, hand palm-down, index finger on the center of their forehead, the other fingers slightly bent. Rada bowed and returned the salute, obviously pleased to be the escort of the new guest. The salute did not seem to be based on authority or rank, but just a friendly way of saying 'hi'.

Rada and Nicholas made their way through the village. At the far end of the village, they entered a structure, through another wooden door. The main room was a sitting room, brightly lit from the windows. The room's floor was made of wood slats and a stone fireplace dominated the left wall. There were two rather comfortable looking chairs in front of the fireplace. On the right wall was a bookshelf holding ancient-looking leather bound volumes, stacked haphazardly with scrolls randomly placed amongst the books. The only other piece of furniture was a round wooden table surrounded by four wooden chairs. Extending from the main room was a smaller area that appeared to be used for food preparation. And finally, there were two small rooms on each side of the "kitchen", each with its own door for privacy. Modern architects would have been impressed by the two internal windows between the main room and the bedrooms. They were made of an opaque glass-like material that let the outside light in but could not be seen through.

Rada said, "Here we are. Lodgings fit for a Magi Initiate. This is where you will be staying. My room is there." He pointed to the left door. "And yours is there," pointing to the right door. "There is a food preparation room in the back for baking bread, and preparing food between our usual communal dining," he added as he pointed to the back center room.

"No Jacuzzi?" asked Nicholas.

"No whakoozee?" questioned Rada. "I'm sorry. I don't understand."

"Oh, never mind. It looks great. I'm starved, can we eat?"

Rada responded smiling, "Of course we can eat! Nourishment at the Cloister is of the essence of everything. I will have some bread and vegetables ready for you shortly. Step into your room and make yourself comfortable. We have provided you with robes so that you may shed your Western clothes. We have a communal bathhouse for your other needs."

"Coed baths..." said Nicholas under his breath.

Nicholas entered his room and looked around. It was simply furnished. He saw a single bed, more like a futon, on one side of the room and an adobe horno fireplace in the far corner. Two off-white robes were folded and laying on the end of the bed.

There was a small desk near the fireplace. On the desk was a leather bound book, an ink well and a feather quill. Nicholas picked up the book and looked at the words on the cover: *The Magi Way, Nicholas Thompson*.

He opened the book and saw that the pages inside were blank.

"Interesting reading."

He flipped through the blank pages.

Rada peaked through the doorway as Nicholas flipped the pages.

"You are to write your instruction manual for becoming a Magi Initiate. The book is blank because you have not yet started training. You will fill it with lessons as you learn them. The words will come to you, you will see. I have already written my Initiate manual and am working on my Novice lessons now."

Nicholas considered this and asked, "I'm writing my own lessons? Isn't that kind of like writing my own exam? I am to teach myself? What more could I learn from me?"

"We all have much to learn from ourselves and from the world around us. You will be getting some instruction for the writing but it is more like a personal dictation," responded Rada poignantly. "Enough for now, come, let us eat. Later, you have an appearance before the Magi Council, before the Grand Silence this evening."

"The what???" said Nicholas, "Grand silence?"

Rada put his index finger up to his pursed lips and whispered, "Shhhhh."

Chapter 13

*The proper function of a government is to make
it easy for the people to do good and difficult
for them to do evil.*

Gladstone

Jen was looking forward to her summer in Washington
D.C., the City of Power, and a place where the elite molded the
future. She had spent last summer interning for a Secretary of
Defense Liaison at the Pentagon and had decided that politics were
not her thing. But being part of a city where the movers and shakers
were exploring new ideas and seeking fresh talent was definitely
drawing her there for at least another summer.

This summer Jen had wanted to try something different.
She had always been interested in communication and had decided
to write her dissertation on some facet of the ability to transfer
knowledge in the world of nano-technology. There was plenty of
work going on with nano-satellites, so she thought that might be an
excellent area to pursue. For twenty-one years, the Washington
Internship Program (WIP) had been placing interns in all fields of
study and assured her that they could find an exciting position for
her within the nation's capital. After declining a few possible
positions that did not interest her, WIP had emailed her with a
perfect opening that had just surfaced. She was to meet with her
new employer in three days.

The almost six-hour flight aboard America West seemed
like twenty. Jen kept thinking about her brother and his journey.
Nicholas was the only family she had left. They had had a typical
brother/sister relationship before their parents had disappeared
and he had become her legal guardian. Nicholas had sacrificed his
professional career to make sure she felt protected, that she studied
hard and had a secure home. He took the teaching position at the
local University to stay in town for Jen.

Last summer, when Jen had her internship at the Pentagon, Nicholas had gone with her to D.C. and performed all around the area, lecturing at magic shops from New York to Virginia, as well as at local magic club assembly meetings, and had included her in his performances. This summer was the first time they had ever really been separated. She guessed it was about time, after all, she was twenty-five. And she had felt guilty that perhaps the reason he was not dating was because of his paternal feelings for her. It was time he stopped putting his life on hold for her; perhaps his separation from her would allow him the freedom to meet someone and move on with his life.

Jen had purposely flown to D.C. several days early prior to registering for her internship; there was so much to see and do. She went to Georgetown first; they had the best Sunday Flea Market. Georgetown was a delightful village full of historic charm and European atmosphere settled on a beautiful waterfront. At the Flea Market every Sunday there was always something for everyone. Jen liked the idea of salvaging someone's trash and giving it new life as a treasure. She found many items she would have liked to purchase, but transportation back home to L.A. kept her buying in check.

At one stall, Jen found a beautiful hand-embroidered burgundy silk Samurai kimono that she felt would be perfect for Nicholas. It felt like him, it even smelled like him. She had to get it. Jen tried to be subtle and not look like she really, really wanted it. But she did really, really want it.

She knew that the first one to speak lost the ability to negotiate, so Jen put the kimono down and started to walk away. The seller, an elderly Asian woman, called her back. "You like?" She held out the kimono.

Jen took it from her, "Yes. It's beautiful. But I'm afraid I cannot afford it, I'm a student."

The Asian woman put the kimono over Jen's shoulders, "You look good."

Jen laughed, "Oh, it's not for me. I was thinking to buy it for my brother."

"I can see you like it. For you…" and she looked around as if someone were listening, "One hundred dollars. It worth much more. I asking eight hundred all morning, but it belong to you for one hundred."

Jen gasped. She knew it was worth much more than one hundred dollars, and her funds were indeed limited, but at such a bargain, "I'll take it!"

The Asian woman nodded graciously, placed the kimono in a grocery bag, and handed it to Jen as she took the crisp one hundred dollar bill. The Asian woman bowed again to Jen.

"Thank you," she smiled.

"No – thank you!" Jen bowed back. She would keep the kimono with her to remind her of Nicholas. She had already started missing him and it had only been one week.

Next, Jen wanted to go downtown to the Smithsonian Institute, with its collection of museums spread out throughout D.C. that took days to visit. Jen had a friend from Santa Fe that had designed and constructed the glass walls of the new National Museum of the American Indian and she decided to make a point this trip, to visit the building.

It was getting well into the afternoon, but Jen had saved some time for the International Spy Museum… dedicated to the field and history of espionage, where she got to see all the unusual spy toys. It was always fun to see if the technology in the spy museum could offer anything adaptable to magic. The world had thought that magicians would be perfect spies and they were often accused of such – they traveled the world, had access to the wealthy and elite, carried trunks of questionable props and magical apparatuses and were above suspicion by the military. Even Houdini had an interesting relationship with the CIA that was still under scrutiny.

Jen was staying with Nicholas' friend, Sansa Do, a Vietnamese-Chinese magician and his wife Tori, a concert violinist, on the border of Maryland. Sansa and Nicholas had grown up together, taking the same martial arts classes and had shared the love of magic. But it was Jen's turn to practice katas with Sansa. He had a large studio; actually it was a converted garage, where they could practice in peace. Sansa and Jen were not as perfect in their mirror image stances, but they executed their movements with the grace and focus of experienced martial artists.

"So, did Nicholas do any research about where he was going and with whom before he left?"

"No," Jen answered, equally apprehensive for Nicholas. "I know he can take care of himself, but... well, you know Nick – when he gets something in his head, he won't shake it loose." She believed 'won't' was indeed the correct verbiage, because he could do anything he put his mind to. It wasn't that he 'couldn't', it was because he 'wouldn't'.

"Can we get a hold of him?"

"Don't think so, I've tried calling him twice since he left. He's somewhere in the mountains over there and you know how cell reception is in the mountains."

Sansa was a mentalist and for some reason this summer, he was worried about Jen. He didn't know why. He couldn't place his finger on the uncomfortable feeling that he was sensing. Maybe he was coming down with a cold and it was nothing. But he was more worried about Jen than Nicholas.

"I'll take you into D.C. tomorrow. I have to pick up some printing I had done for some new brochures. What time's your appointment at WIP?" Sansa asked.

"Two. They said it was a formality for official placement. Shouldn't take too long." Jen swung her right leg toward Sansa's head. He saw it coming and ducked.

"Hey! It'll take a lot more than that to catch me!"

"Wasn't trying to catch you, only hit you... kidding... kidding..." Jen laughed. "I'm looking forward to this summer... and getting to spend some time with you and Tori again."

*   *   *

Sansa dropped Jen off in front of the WIP with a promise of returning in an hour. Jen took her paperwork under her arm and waved as Sansa pulled out into the traffic. There was something about being in D.C. that exhilarated her. The world's decisions were made here, in this town. Or so she thought. She bounded into the WIP office.

An hour later, Jen was waiting for Sansa at the curb in front of WIP. He pulled in and Jen bounced into the car.

"One more stop... if that's okay?" Jen asked.

"Sure – where?"

"I need to get a photo taken, passport size, for an I.D. I have to bring it with me when I start tomorrow. You know a place?" she asked.

Sansa nodded.

*   *   *

The door to Burton's lab suddenly opened and John entered, accompanied by Jen. She wore a photo security tag around her neck that dangled down to her waist. Burton was busy at his computer. John approached Burton and handed him a piece of paper, Jen's resume.

"Jen Thompson, twenty-five, graduate of UCLA 2005, working on her dissertation on network-centric communications also at UCLA. Single. Spent last summer working at the Pentagon," Burton read.

"They managed to get her high level clearance paperwork through so she can join us in the 'hole'," John added.

Burton finally looked up at Jen and John.

"I seem to remember just mentioning to you, John, that we do not need an intern! Are we having communication problems of our own?"

"Communication problems occasionally occur due to miscalculations in the link budgets and/or the amount of noise in the system or perhaps the ERP being less than required for transmission and reception," said Jen with a slight smile.

Burton stared stoically at Jen. And then said, "You think you can hold your own here young lady?"

"I do Dr. Carrier, and I would very much appreciate you giving me a chance to perform."

"Remember the magical assistance you do here is a bit different than the type you do on the surface," said Burton smugly. "Yes, I, too, do a bit of research before anyone even reaches my lab. I know your background Miss Thompson, and truthfully, I just wanted to see if you really wanted the job before I let you on our team."

Burton really did want another intern this summer, and had already secretly chosen Jen as the number one candidate. She had all the requirements to fill the role, and to fit in well with the team. And above all, she seemed to recognize his superiority in the lab. He had made all the arrangements to make sure that she would be the intern they would hire, but he did not want his assistants to know that it was he, Burton Carrier, that was really making these decisions, when they thought it was themselves bringing Jen in as another candidate. It was just his way of hiding his true internal power over the environments under his control.

"So, I'm in?" asked Jen.

"You are. But I must tell you, *do not*, and I repeat, do not turn on any equipment until I so instruct."

"Understood," replied Jen.

"I figured I would give her a tour," said John trying to escape from any further directions for the moment.

"An excellent idea. And take the rest of the day off. I won't be needing you today."

Burton walked toward the door and without looking back said, "Very nice to meet you Ms. Thompson. I am sure this will be a summer to remember."

Chapter 14

> *Men are wise in proportion, not to their*
> *experience, but to their capacity for experience.*

James Boswell

As Nicholas entered the council room of the Magi, the low decibel hum and his connectivity with the others in the room persisted. It felt right. He felt like he belonged, like he was no longer searching for another equation or solution, another magical effect, another sleight-of-hand, or technique of martial arts skill to be mastered. For the first time in his life, he felt like just being was enough. And being here, was all that there was and all that there needed to be. This was a good feeling, to say the least.

The council room of the Magi was another architectural feat holding the spirit of the ether within a rock cloister. The large circular, stone-walled room had a ceiling that rose to a peak in the center. It was difficult to say whether there was a top; the optical illusion made it appear endless. Maybe it was an infinite cone and this room was the center of the universe, thought Nicholas, where the entire universe was controlled from this one room. He looked amusingly for the computer screens… there were none. The eleven members of the council, dressed in monk-like togas, were seated around a long rectangular stone table that could have easily fit eleven more members comfortably. But, there was only one empty wooden carved chair at one end of the table.

Nicholas felt at ease dressed now in the robe that had been provided for him. All the council members sat with their eyes closed, their breathing barely discernable. In front of each council member, was a white ball four inches in diameter. Each of the eleven balls was floating, suspended in the air about six inches off the table. The balls rose and fell slightly as if reacting to the council members' shallow breathing. As the balls changed heights there was an ever-so-slight change in the low decibel tone of the room as well. Everything seemed connected.

Nicholas stood at the open end of the table waiting for direction. He was perfectly content to stand, wait, and watch. The apparent council leader, at the opposite end of the table from Nicholas, finally opened her eyes. The other council members remained with their eyes closed.

The open-eyed Magi spoke.

"Welcome, Nicholas. Please be seated."

Nicholas sat in the empty chair.

"First, we would like to thank you for accepting our invitation to join us here during your brief sabbatical. You are, as we all know, a man of many talents. We assure you, these talents are only the basic tools you will need to complete your education with us. They are your admission criteria."

Nicholas appreciated the academic reference but felt he was in the presence of a being much more deserving than any of the deans he had known in his lifetime. He bowed his head slightly and said, "Thank you."

The Magi continued.

"My name is Tenzin. I serve as the Magi Council Prime. I will play the role of the spokesperson for your lessons and will be your personal tutor. You have much to learn and we have no time to waste."

Nicholas listened and humbly said, "I understand."

Tenzin corrected Nicholas and as she spoke, the floating ball in front of her rose and vibrated erratically.

"I do not believe that you do understand. There is much at risk here and our success *is* based on your understanding. It is of utmost importance that you do, understand."

Nicholas began to apologize, "Sorry, I..." But Tenzin cut him off.

"You do not yet understand Initiate, but you will. Indeed you will."

There was a pause and the ball in front of Tenzin dropped slightly and floated calmly again.

"We are certain that you have many questions regarding our Cloister and who we are. Therefore, before we begin your formal training we would like to give some background on our history, where we came from, who we are, why we are here, and why you have joined us."

Nicholas liked this approach. "Sounds good to me. Right now, I am trying to understand the trick with the balls."

Tenzin smiled.

"I think you know better. You seem to be keeping up your layman's façade. There is no trick or chicanery here, only focus, and exertion of the will. But you will understand more in time. For now, think of it as an exercise in focus."

There was a long pause as the Council Prime apparently redirected her thoughts. The ball in front of her briefly dropped closer to the table as she began her dialogue. The soft decibel hum lowered slightly in pitch as well.

"Zoroaster, was the Magus; the first of the Magi as recorded in your history. He was a prophet in ancient Persia who preached about the eternal cosmic strife between good and evil. His visions produced understandings of the universe that changed the perception of what is reality. One of his premier students was a philosopher mathematician by the name of Pythagoras."

Nicholas responded, "A-squared plus B-squared equals C-squared."

"Precisely," responded Tenzin, "and more, much, much more. He became a disciple of Zoroaster after moving to Babylon.

His previous instruction in science and theology was from the priests of Egypt. Egypt was where he was initiated into the mysteries of the Magi. He was a leading disciple of Zoroaster, and by merging his own philosophies with those of Zoroasterism; he created the doctrines of the Magi. These doctrines became the most secretive and magical texts ever created."

Nicholas queried, "More secret than Houdini's Water Torture Cell?"

"Without a doubt," answered Tenzin calmly and paused for a moment before continuing. "Forty years later, Pythagoras returned to Greece when Zoroaster passed away. His ministry and the first Magi council eventually settled in what would become Italy."

"Hail Caesar," said Nicholas under his breath.

Tenzin acknowledged the interruption. "More like 'Hail Romulus'. Caesar was two hundred years later," she said with a smile.

"Regardless, the training of the Magi entailed severe tests of obedience, endurance and abstinence. After the disciples passed these tests, they lived the next five years in total silence."

Nicholas thought, 'Recovery time.'

Tenzin continued, "This was when the real training began. During this long silence they listened to the instructions and lessons of the Magi council from 'behind the veil', as it was known, but they did not speak, nor did they physically see the council. They were instructed to write these lessons down and formulate their own lesson manual as they proceeded."

Nicholas remembered and asked, "The empty book?"

"The empty book," confirmed Tenzin.

"Nicholas, you will be taught in the same manner. You have already endured severe physical and mental tests to achieve your ranks both in the martial arts and scientific worlds. You too, will be taught in silence, and you will write your interpretations down in your instruction manual."

Nicholas still did not understand, "How will I be instructed in silence?"

Tenzin waited. The balls hovered; the eyes of the other council members remained closed. "The words, as Rada has told you, will come to you. The period lasting from supper until after breakfast, meditation and exercise, is known as the Grand Silence. During this period, you will be instructed and you will write your manual. Your lessons will begin this evening."

"But what ever happened to Pythagoras, the doctrines, and how did you end up here?" asked Nicholas.

"Pythagoras' house in Italy was set on fire. Many believed he and his forty disciples were killed in this fire, but no one knew for sure. This, most certainly, was not true."

"Ah, a cover-up," said Nicholas.

"Pythagoras and three of his disciples escaped the fire. Those were tumultuous times with more turmoil foreseen. They searched for another place that could offer them safety. They found a secure haven here, in the Karakoram Range where they could be alone, self-sufficient, meditative and content. They formed and built what is now known as: The Cloister of the Magi."

"A bit of a trek from Italy," said Nicholas.

"Yes, it was an arduous journey with many adventures, but they, or we, have been here now for over two thousand years."

"Talk about getting away from it all. Has there been no communication with the outside?"

"A few have wandered down to your civilization on occasion, but for the most part, we have remained here to study and master the wonders of the universe. We have been observing your civilization in our own manner. Trust me Nicholas, we are not ignorant. How else would you expect us to be able to speak your language?"

"*Dick & Jane* books from Amazon.com?" responded Nicholas.

Either Tenzin did not understand or ignored the comment.

"We have passed down the way of the Magi for centuries. Similar to the heritage of the Dalai Lama in Tibet, we have always had a Tenzin, and he or she, is the reincarnate of all those Tenzin's that have existed throughout history. I am the sixty-first in a long line of spiritual leaders."

"There is much for you to learn. Unfortunately, we do not have the luxury of having you live with us permanently in order to prepare you for your purpose. Nor do we have the time to teach you all the subtleties of our knowledge in the short time you have with us here. However, you will gather sufficient knowledge throughout your brief training. Your lessons begin this evening."

"What if I fail to learn what you expect of me? And I am a little concerned about my 'purpose' as you call it."

Tenzin responded firmly, "I must tell you that failure is not one of your options. You *will* succeed because we expect of you what you *will* accomplish. That is your purpose, for now." The balls all rose a few inches as she spoke.

Tenzin paused and the balls re-adjusted again.

"We hope you will return to the Cloister again to continue your lessons as a Novice and eventually a Master. But, all of this, only after you have abided by the ways of the Magi in the context of your world as it is today. For now, think not of the future, nor the past. Contemplate the present. It is a gift. That is why we call it, 'the present'." She smiled.

"Understood?" Tenzin stared intently at Nicholas.

"Understood," responded Nicholas.

The balls all began to rise, and then dropped suddenly. The audible hum became louder, deeper. A serious undertone was felt throughout the room.

"You must beware Nicholas," said Tenzin solemnly, "Do not belittle what you are doing here; or what may be your eventual fate. I still sense some doubt in your mind and your understanding. There are other events shadowing the eventual outcome of your instruction. The true effectiveness of your magical abilities will depend on your ability to take these lessons into the context of your own world, outside the confines of the Cloister. The education you acquire here must be effectively applied on the outside. These are the lessons that will change the world, as you know it."

Tenzin slowly closed her eyes. The background noise increased as the balls began to move smoothly in a clockwise fashion from one council member to the next. They rose and circled, faster and further up the cone until they appeared as one extremely fast ball spinning at the top of the cone. The sound was very loud ... until there was a very deep and ominous "BOOM!" which reverberated throughout the room slowly diminishing until there was complete silence. The balls disappeared. The Time was defined and it was Now.

*   *   *

The valley below the Cloister of the Magi was carpeted with soft green grass, sprinkled with boulders and small trees. The sounds of birds and running water were predominant against the sound of the wind and the ever-present low hum. Streams flowed down the valley from waterfalls on either side of the grotto where the Cloister was pocketed. These streams branched into capillaries of brooks trickling on polished stone beds through the grass. At the base of the valley ran a roaring river of milky blue glacial water.

At riverside, watching the water rush by, Rada and Nicholas sat quietly. They had found a pool off to the side and were letting their feet dangle in the extremely cold water, which was flowing down from the mountain glaciers. They both wore their robes.

Nicholas broke their contemplation and silence saying, "You know I could get used to these robes. Heck, it's a lot easier than putting on a tie every day. Very comfortable."

"Comfort is very important, Nicholas. Very important," replied Rada.

Staring at his feet dangling in the water Nicholas asked, "What does Tenzin mean, *'Change the world as I know it'*? What are we talking about here? Re-inventing the light bulb or the World Wide Web?"

Rada smiled.

"No. More like the Infinite Wide Web." He paused and said, "Perhaps you did not notice, we have no light bulbs here."

Rada continued, "The doctrines of Pythagoras talk of an infinite web of life connecting every atom to every other atom. Any change, no matter how subtle, in one atom can be felt by all the others. These lessons teach you how to influence this web of life, but first you must understand who you are and your relationship to the whole."

"Again with the *'Who I am?'*"

"Correction. The Who-You-Are in sympathy with the All-There-Is. This is not an easy task."

Rada continued, "For the past two-thousand years these doctrines have been hidden in these mountains. Tenzin is teaching you, so that you can take this magical wisdom down the mountain and beyond. This could, and will, change everything."

Rada knew that clarity would be coming for Nicholas; at least he hoped so.

"Patience. Now is where we are and now it is time for nourishment. Please join me for dinner."

They rose and began the trek up the hill.

Nicholas was lost in thought. This was a lot for one man to grasp. With all his science and philosophical training, he was not prepared for this. He walked with Rada along the path amongst the wild flowers toward the Cloister. He felt the beauty of the moment and saw the valley and the Cloister for the beauty it possessed. What a remarkable place; a haven of spirituality nestled away from all mankind: it was the true Shambala.

Darkness came to the Cloister first before the rest of the valley, and the juxtaposition of the bright green valley to the dark and shadowy Magi habitat was a bit unnerving. It was like crossing through a veil, from daylight to nighttime; both dimensions visible through the veil. Rada and Nicholas entered the Cloister from the cobbled stone paths under the shadow of the grotto ceiling.

Candelabras burned brightly, illuminating two long tables of twenty people each. The tables were occupied except for two empty seats at one table. The magi, with bowed heads, did not look up as Rada guided Nicholas to sit with him in the empty seats. Despite the entire wall of windows lining the room, the only light came from the flickering candles. Vegetables and bread were served on large platters, and three large bowls of soup were placed in the middle of the tables.

No one spoke.

A bell rang softly twice as a sign for everyone to raise their heads and open their eyes. Nicholas hadn't closed his eyes; he had been unsure what to do next and didn't want to miss any protocol.

As the others raised their heads, Nicholas watched the dinner ritual. Each one, in order, ladled themselves soup before breaking bread and serving themselves vegetables. Rada and Nicholas were last. Nicholas repeated what he had observed; he wanted to make sure he was doing everything correctly. They ate in silence.

Nicholas was tired; he realized it now. He was observing too much, too fast. The food tasted amazing. He could visualize the nourishment coming from the vegetable greens as he chewed and swallowed. He could feel the energy being absorbed into his being, but he was still exhausted.

After dinner, Rada and Nicholas silently walked back to their living space. Rada pointed Nicholas to the desk in his room. Nicholas wanted to go to bed, but he knew what was expected of him. Rada looked firm. Nicholas sat at the desk and opened the book. As Rada left the room and closed the wooden door quietly behind him, Nicholas closed the book and put his head in his hands.

It was silent in the room except for the slight whisper of gently moving air. There were a few lit candles, flames flickering, providing a wonderful eeriness and shadow play on the walls of the room. One candle sat on the desk lighting his work area. Nicholas sighed and looked at the blank book on the desk. He picked up the book again and opened it. The sound of the breeze in the room increased.

Suddenly, he heard a soft breathy feminine voice, "*It is time to begin your lessons.*"

Nicholas nearly jumped out of his chair. He raised his arms in self-defense, sharpened his focus, looked about the room and said, "What the...?"

"*It is time to begin your lessons.*" The voice paused and then continued, "*Are you prepared?*" The voice sounded like Tenzin. Nicholas could identify to whom the voice belonged, but where was it coming from? He looked about the room again. He was alone.

"I'm sorry, prepared for what? To have you talk in my head? This is not quite what I expected."

This wasn't like Charlton Heston on Mt. Sinai talking to the burning bush named John Huston. This was coming from inside him, inside Nicholas Thompson. He could hear the voice, and he could feel an unsettling vibration within his own being.

The voice responded, "*This is the only way to completely personalize your instruction and progress along the path of the Magi. Each* manual is different because of your own personal interpretation of these lessons, and of what You personally hear. These lessons are meant only for you. They mean little to anyone else. Are you prepared to begin?"

"Okay, I guess I'm ready."

"*Good,*" replied the voice.

"*Keep a diary in the blank book of what you hear during each lesson. Let us begin.*"

Nicholas opened the book to the first of the blank pages. He picked up the quill pen and dipped it in the ink well. He thought it was a good thing he had taken calligraphy while pursuing his eastern studies.

Nicholas wrote the words as they came to his mind.

"*The first lesson pertains to the realization of the I. Until a Magi Initiate has awakened to a conscious realization of his actual identity and who he truly is, he is not, and will not be, able to understand the source of his power using the vital energy of the universe.*"

Nicholas listened and wrote, not sure he was absorbing the material. He focused on listening and writing.

"*You must enter into a consciousness where the realization of the real self becomes part of your everyday self, and the realizing consciousness becomes the prevailing idea in your mind, around which your entire thoughts and actions revolve.*"

"*Before one attempts to solve the secrets of the universe without, they must master the Universe within; because they are one.*"

The candle flame on Nicholas' desk blew in synchronicity with the flow of words as if someone were speaking in front of the candle.

"*Vital energy encompasses everything, both animate and inanimate. It unites all that there is. It is through the consciousness of this energy field and the use of the will that the Magi acquire their special abilities. To us however, these are not special. It is our way of life. Without*" *these abilities, we would be crippled, like being blind. These are as much, and more, a part of our being than our physical senses."*

Nicholas wrote quickly but he was truly, very tired. He tried to focus.

"The real self is the divine spark which is part of the sacred flame of the eternal vital energy. It is immortal, eternal, indestructible, and invincible."

As these last words were heard, Nicholas' eyes shut and he was sound asleep before his head hit the desk with a "thud". He did not awaken.

Tenzin said to herself, *"That will be enough for tonight."*

       *   *   *

Below the Cloister, three groups of Magi were performing physical training in the dawn sunlight. Each group had about forty people and approximately fifty feet separated each group. They were all performing a blend of what appeared to be Tai Chi and slow focused Kung Fu-like moves barefoot on the grass, in unison and in silence. One group had an adult leading a group of children who appeared to be in between the ages of about six and twelve. There was a group of adults that was more adept than the children, which included students in their teenage years. The last group of adults appeared much more adept than the others. For their efforts, a black ball floated around each member of this group matching the dance routine that they were performing. Practicing basic moves only, the other group of adults were still beginners. They had apparently not reached the level to be accompanied by any black balls in their routines. Still, the kicks and fluid hand motions on the hillside were poetic in the sense that they interpreted the essence of the feelings and emotions of the moment into an emotional context of physical movements.

Nicholas was intermixed with Rada in the second group. With his martial arts background, it was easy for him to pick up the moves. He held his own. It was an ethereally delicate scene as they practiced movements in unison. Rada looked at Nicholas and smiled. Nicholas smiled back. He was comfortable in this regiment, and felt surprisingly well after last night's late lesson.

After training, Nicholas and Rada walked toward their lodging. It was very quiet; the Grand Silence was still in session. Suddenly there was the sound of a loud 'GONG' ending the noiseless peace.

As if the entire cavern was awakening from a deep slumber, voices and soft whispers were becoming heard throughout the Cloister.

Rada turned to Nicholas and said, "So what do you think?"

Nicholas smiled, and pondered for a moment. He truly felt at peace. The words he had written in regards to Quantum Reality being determined by perception were no longer just words and theory. He was beginning to realize whom he was inside, and becoming aware of his spiritual connection with the universe. He was actually beginning to have a sense of relationship of 'self' to the 'whole', and it felt very good. Very good, and very powerful. So he responded to Rada accordingly, with naught but a smile and a word: "Magical."

Chapter 15

*The real distinction is between those who adapt
their purposes to reality and those who seek to
mold reality in the light of their purposes.*

Henry Kissinger

There had been nothing, not a word from Nicholas for
almost two months now. Jen was beginning to worry about his
well-being. He did warn her that he might not be able to
communicate with her where he was going, but she worried
nonetheless. Certainly after all this time she should have heard
something from him; a postcard, something...

On occasion, Nicholas had been eccentric in his choices, and
she knew well that when he decided to focus on a path, he totally
engulfed himself in the process. However, in this case, she
wondered how engulfed he had become, and when she would hear
from him again. She could imagine some monastic cult hidden
away in the mountains brainwashing her gullible brother. Okay, he
was not that gullible, but she wondered where the heck he could be.
She amused herself with visions of bumping into Nicholas at an
airport in an orange robe, handing her a flower and asking for a
donation. She knew better, of course, nevertheless her conniving
imagination had managed to rent some space in her head and was
going rampant with a variety of alternatives. She hoped she would
hear from him soon.

The job at Mount Weather had become just that, a job. It
was an internship; so basically, she did all the grunt work. It wasn't
as promised, an exciting Cryptographic endeavor, but grunt work.

In addition, since the team didn't have time between
experiments to mentor and train her, they had done what all good
science and engineering teams do with a new hire: they gave her a
cubicle with a desk, a red classified phone for classified

conversations, a computer, and at least one thousand pages of documentation to digest in the first few weeks.

The documentation was not along the lines of an instruction manual, but a series of in-depth specifications on quantum computing algorithms and more specifications about the system. Her mind drifted constantly while reading. Two pages of reading and her eyes would slowly close. She fought to stay awake and to comprehend the material.

Her only redemption was, that since she was still the newbie; she was also assigned the menial tasks, but tasks that nonetheless fulfilled her desire to be helpful in the grand scheme of things. She compiled the Excel spreadsheets for the experiments, and couriered requests for additional support equipment to the appropriate signatories as directed. At least these tasks kept her awake, and allowed her to meet more people throughout the facility. She knew her contributions, however menial, meant something to the government and to science, and for that reason, even the tedium was more than acceptable.

Jen actually cared about national security. She was a patriot and felt very privileged to be privy to such important aspects of the United States security efforts. The bonus for her was that she cared even more about the science behind the research and was truly fascinated with Dr. Carrier's theories.

What Jen did not care for was Dr. Carrier personally; he was rude, self-involved, barked orders and treated his full-time employees with a loathing she found hard to ignore. She knew he was a genius with no people skills, so it was fortunate for her that she didn't have to spend much time directly under his supervision.

Overall, she was positive about the situation. She was hopeful that she would eventually become a more integral member of the team.

But everything was about to change. Burton barked at his assistants to meet him in the conference room immediately.

"I am putting the Temporal Quantum Entanglement Experiment on hold," he said as the team of four sat at the conference table.

"Continuing to experiment without the correct formulations for success will most certainly fail. However, while I focus on re-calculating the quantum relationships within the formulas, I want to proceed with another experiment. This will be an experiment in Quantum Telepathy."

They had the highest regard for Burton's intellect and theories but this one seemed a bit beyond the norm, even for Burton.

"I know you're all wondering how many quantum martinis I have been drinking. I can tell you, none."

He waited for a laugh.

They stared at him awaiting the explanation.

"This experiment is being done in a variety of different institutions, highly reputable institutions by the way, around the world. Innsbrook dabbled in it and obtained success in Quantum Teleportation. Very highly regarded professors in the United Kingdom are on a path for success in this area. It is known as 'Social Telepathy,' and is very similar to the telepathy used by the social groups of closely knit teams such as birds or ants."

They looked at him wondering: Why were they being compared to birds and ants?

"You see we have an advantage in this capacity in respect to the other institutions that are investigating this phenomenon. We are trapped here, beneath the earth for sometimes days at a time in very close quarters, a sub-group of human society. This is the perfect place to conduct the research."

He paused, and then continued, "Our new team member, Jen, will be the ideal subject for the experiment." Jen was immediately interested. She was being asked to participate as a member of the team and Quantum Telepathy would fit into her dissertation focus as well.

John and Harold stared at Jen and she smiled and shrugged her shoulders agreeably. Regardless of how the choice was made, she was happy she would be getting a new opportunity. Anything would be better than more death-by-documentation. This was a step in the right direction.

'Here we come Social Telepathy,' she thought.

"We'll start the experiment this afternoon. Beginning tomorrow, we'll conduct the Quantum Telepathy, QT, experiments first thing everyday. That will leave us the balance of the day to review our data and to continue our efforts on the Quantum Entanglement experiment."

They went into their hyper-attentive listening mode.

"The experiment will be performed as follows: Jen will be placed in the sealed room where we had placed the reception device for the quantum communication experiment. She will be alone, with nothing to distract her. I will be placed in the other SCIF behind my office, which no one else has access to. I will write one sentence on a piece of paper every morning. I will turn all of my attention to that phrase, and focus on the meaning of what I wrote. Jen will close her eyes and try to establish a telepathic connection with my mind through, what I believe, is a type of social quantum entanglement of our minds. It will be the proof that we are one, or all part of one another."

Dr. Carrier's three employees were beginning to wonder if the failure of the communication experiment had actually affected Burton's scientific judgment. This sounded absurd. Nevertheless, this was Dr. Carrier, and some of the other successful experiments that John and Harold had participated in with him were pretty darn farfetched initially. Jen, on the other hand, was beginning to wonder whether she should go back to reading documents in her cubicle.

"Initially, I do not expect any definitive results. But I want to give this a try." He paused and decided to open up a bit. "Have you ever been stuck at a red light and glanced over at the car next to you and immediately seen the head of the passenger or the driver turn to meet your eyes?"

They looked at him and slowly nodded their heads, and said, "yes," with some trepidation.

"Why is that? How did they know you were looking? Hmmm," he said while looking at the ceiling with a slight smile. "How do birds know when to turn in unison while flying in a flock? How do ants communicate the disturbance in one area of their efforts to another almost immediately? It is instantaneous. Kind of like Quantum Entanglement, huh?"

He let his employees ponder these questions for a moment before continuing, "I believe there is a universal consciousness for living beings, formed within social organizations and perhaps even beyond. It is a quantum relationship that may have actually originated during the Big Bang along with the origin of the universe. Everything is connected. This is what I want us to delve into."

There was a long pause as they all sat looking at Dr. Carrier. At that moment, they all realized how far their lives had progressed since their childhood days when they would grow colored crystals on kitchen counters or build volcanoes for fourth grade science projects. They were in the midst of discovering and potentially understanding all.

"While Jen and I perform our little experiment, I expect you, Harold, and you, John to be working out the formulas for how this relationship could be established in quantum theory."

John and Harold glanced at each other with a look. Where would they start? What was the baseline equation or relation to work from? What were the boundary conditions? Of course, they had been there before. This was how all-good experiments testing the margins of existence began.

"So the time to begin is now. Day one is today," said Burton in a tone similar to Rod Serling's of the Twilight Zone.

Chapter 16

> *We are so anxious to achieve some particular*
> *end that we never pay attention to the psycho-*
> *physical means whereby that end is to be*
> *gained. So far as we are concerned, any old*
> *means is good enough. But the nature of the*
> *universe is such that ends can never justify the*
> *means. On the contrary, the means always*
> *determine the end.*
>
> *Aldous Huxley*

Quill in hand, Nicholas wrote intensely. He was no longer tired during his lessons each night and would have liked them to go on longer.

Tenzin's voice was heard in his head and he wrote, *"They can who know they can. The Magi's character is a perfectly educated will."*

Nicholas nodded as he wrote quickly.

"Nothing can resist the will of a man who knows what is true and wills what is good. Within you is a power, part of the living force, which, the more you trust and learn to use, will allow you to prevail over the essence of all matter."

"The universe is a great organism, controlled by a dynamic psychical order. By developing the will of the Magi, we can learn to influence that order and control our own reality."

"For now we are done."

Nicholas felt sleepy about the time Tenzin finished the dictation. He put his quill down and moved over to his bed. He remained focused on his reality and his will. Now he willed himself to sleep to nourish his body and mind. His soul had been fed.

*　　　　　*　　　　　*

The following morning, Nicholas and Tenzin sat beneath a beautiful mountain oak tree in the valley of the Magi. They faced one another, cross-legged. Tenzin held in her hand one of the white balls first seen floating in Nicholas' first meeting at the council.

Tenzin spoke softly with direction, "Close your eyes, Nicholas."

Nicholas closed his eyes.

"Can you tell me now with your eyes closed, where is your mind? Where are the walls of your mind? How big is your mind?"

Nicholas responded with his eyes shut, "There are no walls, there is no apparent limit. With my eyes closed, my mind is all there is."

Tenzin smiled.

"Exactly! Your mind is everywhere. There is no confinement within your skull; it is all there is, and it is infinite."

The ball in Tenzin's hand rose and circled around her body and head once and then began to circle Nicholas' head, keeping a distance of about one foot, while his eyes remained closed.

"Now focus on your mind space. Can you sense anything?" asked Tenzin.

Nicholas concentrated and said, "No, it seems empty... No wait, there does seem to be something."

The ball slowed its rotation and dropped in elevation.

"There is something, like a movement ... uh ... it seems like a circular feeling around ... wait I've got it. It is like a marble-in-a-funnel feeling and ... no ... yes ... I can really sense it now. I can feel it!" He said excitedly.

The ball rose more.

"I think it's actually part of my mind. I can control it. I can feel it."

The ball started to move substantially faster now.

"It's moving faster now. Can you tell?"

Tenzin smiled, "Yes, I can tell." She paused and then continued, "Why don't you try and stop it."

Having fun, Nicholas responded, "Okay, I can do that."

"Let's see, slow down…"

The ball slowed down slightly.

"And … STOP!"

The ball froze immediately between Tenzin and Nicholas.

"How'd I do?"

"Open your eyes," said Tenzin.

Nicholas opened his eyes and saw the ball frozen between them. He was surprised yet calm and focused.

He smiled, "Hmmm. So there was a marble in my mind-funnel. Pretty cool. Well, nobody can say that Magi don't have balls. Even the girls do."

Tenzin remained serious and did not smile.

"But could you say that there was a ball before you opened your eyes? Could you say definitely?"

Nicholas thought for a moment and responded, "I could feel it with my mind and control it with my will. It may not have been a real ball in my mind until I opened my eyes, but if it were only a wave pattern, I still controlled the waves. Perhaps I collapsed it to a physical ball when I opened my eyes."

"Perhaps," said Tenzin. "Perhaps though, physical reality was already established before you opened your eyes, and your mind had a grasp on the ball's wave relation to your energy field, rather than the solid form."

Nicholas was now confused, "Sorry but could you repeat that, like in a language that a mere astrophysics professor could understand?"

Tenzin sighed, "There is no need for you to over analyze the physics right now. You need to understand your mind's abilities. You will develop your own theories of the physics, I am sure, in the future."

"For now, let it suffice to say you are progressing extremely well. You should be pleased."

"I am pleased, but I really want..."

Tenzin held her index finger to her mouth and said "Shhhhh" as the gong rang three times signaling another beginning of the Grand Silence. Nicholas sighed in frustration. Tenzin rose and the white ball encircled her slowly. She beckoned Nicholas to join her and they walked up the hill towards the Cloister, the ball encircling them both. Student and teacher were cocooned in a magical silence.

Chapter 17

Satan merely represents a force of nature - the powers of darkness which have been named just that because no religion has taken these forces out of darkness. Nor has science been able to apply technical terminology to this force. It is an untapped reservoir that few can make use of because they lack the ability to use a tool without having to first break down and label all the parts which make it run. It is this incessant need to analyze which prohibits most people from taking advantage of this many faceted key to the unknown-which the Satanist chooses to call "Satan".

Anton Szandor LaVey

In the darkness, a solitary flame rose from a red candle. A figure was dressed in a long black robe with a hood drawn over his head; his face obscured. This sorcerer of science understood the implications of the quantum world and he believed he could create the reality of the black magic he was performing. He understood that believing was seeing. He was Burton Carrier, and always would be, but tonight he was also a wizard of the dark arts communicating with what he believed to be, pure evil.

Prostrate, he came before the candle and chanted words in Enochian. According to legend, Enochian was an ancient language passed on to humans by the Enochian Angels in the 1500's. The truth was it was much older than the 1500's; many sects employing black magic had used this language. The Satanic Bible had thirteen commandments, all listed in Enochian. But its true origin was unknown.

Burton raised and lowered his arms toward the flame as he spoke, *"Ol sonuf vaoresaji gohu IAD Balata, elanusha caelazod."*

The flame began to flicker to the rhythm of his arm movements. He fanned the flames, and they began rising above his head. "*Sobrazod-ol Roray I ta nazodapesad, GIRAA TA MAELPEREJI! CORAXO CAHISA COREMEPE BAELZEBUB!*"

As these last words were enunciated, the flames from the candle erupted and a form arose within the flames. Surrounded by flame, and transparent except for a visible outline, the form was a creature, part flame, part reptile, part demon: all bad. The creature began to take a visible shape. Its eyes were slanted and filled with dark orbs, like those of a shark. It had two huge horns protruding from its head, curling upwards and to the side. Dangling at either side of the form were short lizard-like legs, with three thin scrawny fingers and needle-like claws. It spoke:

"Ah, Dr. Carrier we meet at last. I am Anan'kra."

Burton stared at the creature. This was not what he expected.

"I understand. This is not the scientific communication you anticipated. Truthfully, it is very scientific. You have followed our directions perfectly. The language you spoke, Enochian, was our civilization's language. We passed it down to your people many centuries ago. There is a connection between its use and the ability to communicate telepathically with our people. We have used this to assist others throughout your civilization's history when they called with an open heart, and a giving soul."

The creature smiled craftily.

"This is only in your mind's eye. I am not standing before you. I am communicating telepathically as we have done with beings on your planet for thousands of years. There are Others who are ready to help you in your endeavors. You are, however, *the key*, because you have the ability through your experiments to talk to us in the past, as well as now, in the present. You can change the future and maybe, even the past. You have a direct link with our own communication devices through your computers and to all of our own sentient devices. However, the Others have been gathering for the storm. You will lead the Others, yourself and us to victory. We will work with you using both this mental focus exercise, known to some as 'black magic,' and with the quantum communication device you have created. We will use the computers to transfer what you need to prepare for our arrival and for you and your supporters to begin your rise to power."

"The Others who represent us within your civilization will help you along your path to power. I will provide remote tutelage through our correspondence, beginning tonight. I have not been participating personally in the history and evolution of the Earth as of late, and have found that the time is now, for me to take a vested interest in both your rise to power and the demise of your enemies. We are pleased. You are a worthy recruit for the preparations of the Coming."

Burton was appreciative but skeptical; 'what did this mean?' "Thank you," he said bowing his head.

'Was he going to be in power, or only a servant to this beast before him?'

He was trying to wrap his mind around these concerns.

'Could this creature read his thoughts? Did Anan'kra know he wanted total power, not just a piece of the power pie? He must mask his thoughts. He must be careful.'

"Do not thank me, Dr. Carrier. You are the one who will be thanked. It is your continued curiosity, ingenuity, and ambition that have assisted in us in finding you. It is your own quest for power and our quest to return to power that will make our symbiotic relationship a success. We are aware of turmoil and the need for a solution."

"There will be a new Leviathan in this world. There have been Others before you: Cleopatra, Pontius Pilate, Genghis Khan, Dr. John Dee, and Adolf Hitler to name but a few. Your quest for fortune and control is great. Our computer connections have allowed me to do much research, and our mental connections prove

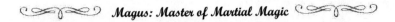

to me that you have the potential and the desire. Do not thank me. Thank *you.*"

The Creature paused again.

"The Others who will assist you on your crusade are spread across the globe. The worthy ones are expecting the coming, but have based their faith on the words of their forefathers, and periodic communications with us. They are pulling together resources to eradicate a potential threat to our efforts. It will soon be time for them to hear from you, and they will search you out. But first, we must have you take control of all available resources, both those of your government, and even more importantly, the mental resources within your own being. All is falling into place. It is time for your training to begin."

Chapter 18

*Power, like a diamond, dazzles the beholder,
and also the wearer; it dignifies meanness; it
magnifies littleness; to what is contemptible, it
gives authority; to what is low, exaltation.*

Caleb Colton

Two weeks later, Jen realized how much the experiment had been an escape from the tedium of her previous assignment. It took half an hour each morning and so far, she had not even gotten close to 'guessing' or 'telepathing' the phrase Burton concentrated on each morning. But, it was a nice break from the reading.

John and Harold had made progress on some nebulous relational hand-waving type of equations, interpreted by some blind cold-fusion scientists in Utah as true quantum telepathic formulas. Hey, they were happy they had written anything down.

Regardless, today for her was just another day in 'the hole.'

Jen stepped into her solitary environment in the entangled reception office and sat in the single chair in the middle of the room, facing the observation window. She hadn't been drinking her usual three cups of coffee these days since Burton thought the caffeine might affect her focus. He thought that sitting alone on a chair in a bright room after drinking three cups of coffee would induce memories of Alan Sheppard sitting in a space suit on top of a rocket and asking if he could urinate.

This morning she sat quietly with her eyes closed and focused on her breathing. She knew that Dr. Carrier was in his own space focusing on the phrase before him, but she had decided not to fret. She would relax and see if anything came to mind.

It had been a great two weeks. The whole team, or at least the three assistants, had become much closer. They had lunch and dinner together most days and began spending every evening in the

Mount Weather facility in each other's company, a quarter a mile beneath solid rock. Sansa and Tori were out of town touring with their show, so there was no reason for Jen to rush home.

Most evenings they played poker in the office. Burton said poker might be conducive to the experiment, as they tried to interpret bluffs and envision what cards the other members of the team held in their hands; kind of like the ESP tests with the Zener cards with stars, circles and wavy lines on them. 'Who really knew?' she thought, but it certainly had made them a much closer team; at least John, Harold and Jen.

Jen was learning to accept Burton, who usually left the office around nine o'clock every evening. He said he had his own calculations to continue with, for the quantum communication experiment and late evening status correspondence he needed to provide every night. Jen wondered who the heck he would be giving status reports to since they were truly autonomous from the other sectors in the division, but she saw how John and Harold truly appreciated Burton's dedication. Burton had seemed more and more distant, more self-involved and quicker to reach his anger state if something did not go his way.

As Jen sat alone in her room, Burton contemplated the situation and the plan forward. He had not written his phrase down yet. Once he did, he wanted to be able to totally focus on the phrase. Lately his mind was all over the universe, multi-tasking his neural networks, taxing his ability to concentrate.

Burton was excited with the concept of realizing the power his ambition could give him. But he was nervous about the execution of the plan. The creature had communicated a very detailed plan that would change the world, as he knew it. It had been Burton's dream and now he was the instigator; the authority responsible to make the plan happen. He saw the result of the plan in his mind and he was very pleased.

He scribbled down an Enochian phrase that would be very easy to verify if Jen were to receive any message telepathically.

"Coraxo cahisa coremepe, od belanusa Lucala azodiazodore paebe Soba," he repeated to himself. This was a simple phrase he focused on since he had been using the Enochian chants to concentrate his will when communicating with Anan'kra in real-time. He remembered Anan'kra saying that this phrase was part of the tenth Enochian key. It translated roughly, 'The thunders of wrath doth slumber in the North.' He thought this very appropriate, since he envisioned the North as the realm of Anan'kra. He was prepared to awaken the slumbering North and impart their wrath on the world. He had a great vision of conquest and dissolution firmly fixed in his mind's eye.

In the isolation room, Jen jumped as if hit by an electric shock from the chair beneath her. Her eyes snapped open wide as the lightning bolt of telepathic energy struck her mind. She became temporarily blinded to her surroundings and instead saw a fast-frame montage of images: a nuclear Navy warship USS Nimitz, air traffic control tower in chaos, an electrical grid for a large populated city shut down, a satellite careening in space, a microwave tower meltdown, all popping through her mind as fast as paparazzi's bulbs flashing. The Enochian words in her cerebellum were readable. It was overwhelming, exhausting, a sense of total devastation filled her mind. The vision had only taken a second and it was done; leaving her scared, scared beyond belief. She felt as if she had been hit in the head with a rubber mallet. Her head throbbed intensely, and then slowly the pain subsided as her vision returned, leaving only the memory of the horrible images.

John and Harold barged into the room. They had been observing her as she changed from a calmly breathing subject to an anxious, bright-eyed, apparently shocked and horrified victim.

"Are you okay?" they said in unison.

She was dazed, but coherent. "Yes, I... I think so. Sorry, I must have fallen asleep and had a nightmare," she lied, but knew for now this was best.

"Oh... okay..." said John, a little unsure. "Boy, you scared us. You must have jumped a foot out of your chair."

"Yeah, I have a history of night terrors. My body must be reacting to the lack of coffee. I was too relaxed."

"Let's call it quits for today," said John.

'Quits...' she thought, 'yeah that's a good idea. Let's call it quits and like really quit. Let's run for the hills 'cause this is gonna be some heck of a week!'

Burton collided with John and Harold as he pushed them aside to get to Jen. "What happened?" demanded Burton, searching her face as if to detect any clue as to what she had just experienced. "Did you hear anything?" Jen shook her head no.

"What did you see?"

"It was so fast."

"Did you see images? Words? What?" he demanded angrily.

"I think I may have dozed off and had a nightmare. There were these flashes of light but I don't know what they meant. No words... I don't know. Sorry," she looked into his eyes and began to cry. She knew he suspected more, but instead of questioning her further, he changed the subject.

"Well, we've been working too late. I know I've been pushing you very hard. For the next two days, you take time off. Get some rest, some sunlight," he said with what appeared to be friendly consideration. This wasn't like Burton.

Jen knew better.

"But ..." John started to say.

"No buts. I am declaring the next two days a Burton Carrier holiday; a paid vacation for all three of you. I know you have been busting your butts. So take some time off. That is an order!"

'A Burton Carrier holiday,' Jen thought. 'Yeah right, a vacation from us so he can work alone.' She saw what he was planning and it terrified her.

He finished with, "I can guarantee, when you return, that you will have a fresh new look at the world," he paused, "really."

Chapter 19

> *The school should always have as its aim that the young man leave it as a harmonious personality, not as a specialist. The development of general ability for independent thinking and judgment should always be placed foremost, not the acquisition of special knowledge.*

Albert Einstein

Nicholas sat in a lotus position on top of the futon bed in his room. His arms were extended over his knees, palms upward, middle finger and thumb touching. He was meditating tangit style, opening his chakras and allowing the energy to flow freely throughout his body. A low hum was audible, but not the same as Nicholas had heard before, because this time it was coming from him as if he were chanting. But he was not, at least not audibly. He had been continuing to write in the evenings whether he had a voice in his head or not. He wrote his own personal annotations to the lessons he had learned and scribed. He found that when he started the evening in meditation, his writing flowed more clearly.

This evening was no different. The voice had not yet begun the lesson so he was meditating. Suddenly a sharp pain pounded in his skull, he grabbed his head and yelled, "OW!"

"What was that? Tenzin, are you in my head?" he yelled to no one.

Tenzin responded calmly in the mind of Nicholas, *"No, it was not I."*

"One of the council elders?" questioned Nicholas.

"I believe you are empathizing with someone else. Anyone can freely communicate with you if they are of the same vibration."

Nicholas grimaced and said, "Well, ow!"

Tenzin responded, *"You must be careful. All who interfere may not be positive. You must learn to protect yourself from negative interference without closing off your own energy. Regardless, it is necessary for us to continue, and for us to conclude."*

Nicholas got up from the futon and sat down at the desk. He opened his book and picked up his pen. Tenzin began, *"Wherever you go, wherever you are, THERE is the Center of your World. YOU are and always will be the center of your existence, and all that is outside, revolves around you as its center. Understanding this is the completion of the road to initiation on the path to becoming a Magi. We think we have now given you the key to the first stage of the path. Let us conclude these lessons by quoting one of the old Magi Masters: 'When the soul sees itself as a center surrounded by its circumstances, as the sun knows that it is a sun, and is surrounded by its whirling planets, then it is ready for the wisdom and power of the Magi'."*

She paused, and then said with finality, *"That is all."*

Nicholas finished writing and placed his quill in its holder. He blew his breath slowly and deliberately across the page to accelerate its drying.

'Why?' he thought. 'There is no reason to hurry. The ink will dry in time. Is it really my duty to accelerate the process? Perhaps not. But perhaps, my influence on the universe around me is my responsibility. It is the knowledge of my place and influence within the universe that I have been made aware. Perhaps assisting in the drying ink is my responsibility. Well,' he considered, 'at least it is my privilege to know that I can influence the process.'

Nicholas felt complete.

*　　　*　　　*

In the council room of the Cloister, Nicholas sat at the table with the council elders. Tenzin sat at one end with Nicholas at the other. She and Nicholas were the only ones with their eyes open. A single ball floated before each of them, including Nicholas.

Tenzin spoke with a sense of pride, "Your training as a Magi Initiate is nearly complete. You have excelled far beyond our greatest expectations."

"Thank you for all of your patience and wisdom. I know I have not been your typical student, and very much appreciate all you have taught me this summer, which by the way, feels more like three years, not three months," replied Nicholas.

"There are many more lessons to come, but first you must take what you have learned back to your world to continue to learn and to begin to influence others."

Tenzin stared intently at Nicholas and continued, "Albeit we would prefer to have you stay with us and continue your training in the cloister, there are Others outside who have begun an alternative path which must be corrected. It will be your task to right those that have wandered by using your abilities as an Initiate. Again, I must caution you. Beware of negative interference. There are many battles on the horizon, but you can prevail. You are our hope, our prodigal son, who will bring the true Magic to humanity."

Tenzin paused. A tear slowly rolled from the corner of her eye. "I will miss your spirit's presence in our halls but you must take your leave now."

Solemnly, Nicholas said, "I will miss you as well."

Tenzin responded with a slight smile, "Well, not to worry, I am sure we will be 'in touch' so to speak. Now, be off on your journey down the mountain, and may you fare well on your magical path."

*   *   *

Nicholas packed his possessions, including his lesson book into his backpack as Rada watched. He left his robes folded at the foot of his futon, dressed in his Western clothing and slung the heavy snorkel-tundra jacket over his shoulder.

Rada and Nicholas left the Old Wing of the Cloister with four yaks. They stopped before the exit to the outside of the mountain; neither wanted to begin the ritual of farewell. They stood facing each other as their torches began to flicker from the hidden winds passing through the door from the outside. Finally Rada spoke, "Well, I will miss you Dr. Nick." He paused and looked down, "I will miss you a lot."

Nicholas placed his torch in a holder by the door and hugged Rada, "I will miss you too, Rada. You have been a great partner along the path, a good friend and a brother."

"I did not get to learn about 'light bulbs'," said Rada.

"I will be back, and the next time, I will teach you about my world. Maybe one day you will come down off this mountain for a visit. What do you think?"

Rada smiled and said, "Maybe one day!"

Nicholas pushed the huge heavy door open and stepped out into the cold wind of the western face of the mountain. He turned quickly back to Rada and hugged him again. A sharp pain hit Nicholas and he grabbed his head and groaned in response. As he stepped away from Rada, he stared deeply into Rada's eyes.

He realized two things immediately: Number One, someone else outside the Cloister was indeed trying to get into his mind; Number Two, he believed that Rada would be a tremendous asset on his journey back into civilization. Rada would reinforce his connection to the Cloister, and Nicholas realized he was going to need all the help he could get.

Nicholas' head was still pulsing.

Rada smiled. He was formulating a mental equation and proposing a solution, not for the origin of the cosmos, but for

125

Nicholas' potential symbiotic existence with Rada's own. "I don't want you to go off alone," Rada declared.

With complete understanding, Nicholas replied, "Exactly. Why don't you take a leave from the Cloister? The best way to improve your knowledge of the world is to spend some time in it. I can get you a student VISA and you can join me in the United States. We can return to our studies here at the Cloister after a year." Nicholas paused and then said, "Call it a study abroad."

Rada looked apprehensive, "Well, I am not quite sure I am prepared to travel beyond the Cloister."

Nicholas responded confidently like a professor, "You'll do fine. There is no better time than the present to begin your studies of the world."

Rada pondered the decision, but he knew the answer, "It looks like I must. Now is the time." He looked to Nicholas for reassurance, "And you will be my tutor?"

"And I will be your tutor."

"Done," responded Rada with finality. "Done."

Nicholas smiled and repeated, "Done."

Chapter 20

*For certain is death for the born
And certain is birth for the dead;
Therefore over the inevitable
Thou shouldst not grieve.*

Bhagavad Gita

Being outside was a far cry from the warm haven of the Cloister. Rada was clad in heavy fur coats and boots he had assembled from the Cloister. He appeared as a blend of a large 'tribble' and a Kodiak bear. Snow fell heavily as Nicholas and Rada trod down the path in an atypical end-of-summer blizzard. At his spiritual core, Rada knew he had made the right choice to follow Nicholas. He knew Nicholas needed the help and that there was confrontation in the near future which he needed to support. The council had always thought it would be best for Rada and Nicholas to travel together back into society, but wanted them to make the final decision. Fate could be encouraged, but the ultimate decision needed to be made by the ones experiencing the reality of their decisions.

While it seemed like a great idea at the time, Rada had begun to feel uneasy. He knew his fears would soon pass and they would be in America together. But there was definitely something else that made him uncomfortable. Maybe it was the blizzard and the cold that were disrupting his usual sense of comfort. Maybe.

They were heading south from the mountains to Skardu, capital of Baltistan. Skardu was one of the two major hubs for all trekking expeditions in the northern area of Pakistan; a region that included four of the fourteen Eight-thousander peaks (8,000m and higher) of the world. This area had hosted many mountaineering travelers. Nicholas and Rada planned to find one of the two roads that led from the Askole and Hushe Valleys to Skardu. These valleys were the main entrances to the snowy giants in the Karakoram, and to the huge glaciers of Baltoro, Biafo, and Trango.

Treks to the highest plateau in Pakistan, known as the Deosai Plains, either started from, or ended at, Skardu. At a height of about thirteen thousand five hundred feet these were some of the highest plateaus of the world, second only to Tibet. Access to these mountains made Skardu a major summer tourist hotspot with hotels, restaurants, bars and shops and way too many people.

The piercing cold was relentless. Visibility was so poor, Rada strained to see Nicholas walking in front of him. He could barely see Nicholas' footprints in the snow and hung on to the reins of the yak to steady himself. The cold froze every cell of exposed flesh; any place the skin touched the air was prone to frostbite. They wore heavy gloves on their hands and wraps over their faces to cover their noses and protect their lungs from the freezing cold.

Whatever monotony Nicholas had endured ascending the mountain with Ahura, it was worse on the descent. And truly, it was not monotonous as much as it was just a very difficult trek. The whistling wind prohibited dialogue and all they could do was put one foot in front of the other and plod down the mountain. Their only goal was to reach Skardu as quickly as possible.

The wind howled so loudly that Nicholas and Rada did not hear the muffled 'pop' sound behind them. One of their four yaks stopped suddenly and dropped to the ground with a barely audible thud. Nicholas and Rada looked at each other puzzled before they were able to piece together what had actually happened.

The yak had been shot.

Warm red blood seeped from underneath the yak's body, staining the white snow crimson red.

Nicholas and Rada both turned away from the pummeling wind to face the perpetrators. Blurred by the spiraling snow, it was difficult to see the four horses that were carrying the four men with rifles. Nicholas' first thought was that these men might be soldiers in the war between Pakistan and India. They were obviously not traveling salesmen; their arsenal of weapons and their demeanor belied that concept. They each had packs tied to their horses, one of which actually appeared to be alive and struggling.

One of the four men yelled in broken English, "Yaks. Want yaks!"

Rada and Nicholas looked at each other, and Nicholas yelled back, "So do we." But he also knew that didn't make sense. If they truly did want the yaks, why had they shot one?

Another man raised the barrel of his rifle and focused his sight on Nicholas. He took aim, and fired. Nicholas and Rada dove to the left and right of their yaks as the bullet missed its mark and was lost in the snow. They rolled into the whiteness of the blizzard and buried themselves quickly in the soft snow, becoming invisible. Between the wind and the blizzard conditions, it was not hard to become quickly hidden.

The four horsemen charged forward searching for Nicholas and Rada. The horses reacted nervously as they approached the area where the men were buried. A ball of snow hit one of the horses in its muzzle, and the horse startled. It reared and dumped the large struggling pack off its back. The wrapped captive fell to its knees and forward onto its face in the snow, continuing to wiggle, while the horseman tried desperately to regain control of the frightened horse.

Rada reached deep in the snow for some harder pieces of ice, and packed snow around these into very solid snowballs. These snowballs were the size of baseballs and as hard as rocks as they hurled through the air and pelted each of the horsemen in the head and body. As fast as he could make them, he was throwing them at the attackers with his mind. His aim was meticulous. The horsemen fought to stay on their horses as the snowball barrage continued. The horses twisted and pranced, trying to escape the ice-balls.

Nicholas used one of the bulky bodies of a yak as a shield, and crawled towards the horsemen. He pulled himself up from beneath one horse. As the horse and rider pivoted in the mayhem, Nicholas reached up and grabbed the rifle from the horseman. He pulled the marauder off the horse and whacked him in the head with the butt of the rifle.

Rada continued quickly packing the deadly snowballs, and hurling them with his mind, not his arms, as fast as he could pack them together; his aim was very adept.

Nicholas side-kicked a second horseman off his horse as a third horseman swung his rifle at Nicholas. Swiftly, Nicholas blocked the barrel with the barrel of the rifle he had already confiscated. He swung his rifle around and rifle butted the third horseman off the horse. With one marauder on either side of him, Nicholas used all his martial arts training to overpower both men to the ground. They were already dazed and confused from all the ice-balls to the head, and instead of shooting them, he used the rifle in his possession as a 'Bo' and knocked them both senseless into the snow.

Rada sailed a large snowball at the remaining marauder that hit him squarely in the forehead. It was dead-on, right between the eyes. The assailant dropped unconscious to the snow. The four horsemen were scattered on the ground, their horses prancing and pawing above them in the blizzard.

Nicholas yelled into the wind, "Rada, tie them up. I want to see if the prisoner is still alive." He motioned to Rada tying an invisible knot in the air and communicating with his mind, in case he hadn't heard.

Rada nodded. He removed some rope from one of the saddles.

Nicholas pulled the captive up from the snow. He removed the wrap around the head. The face beneath the fabric was soft, and tanned. The captive was a woman and she appeared to be a very beautiful woman; unconscious but alive. Nicholas replaced the wrap around her head to keep her protected from the wind and cold, and carried her to one of the horses. He placed her on the horse and tied her hands to the saddle so she could not fall off again. Her head rested against the horse's neck.

Rada had finished tying up the third horseman. As he was dragging the third one to the other two, the fourth prisoner roused and reached into his tunic. He extracted a handgun. He saw Nicholas tie the woman to a horse, raised his arm and pointed his gun. As Nicholas turned from the horse, Rada heard the wind-deadened 'pop' and yelled, "No!" into the storm. There was a flash and smoke trailed out from the pistol. Rada saw the bullet exit the gun's barrel and fly through the snowflakes. In his minds-eye, he saw the slow motion journey of the projectile. There was nothing he could do as the bullet entered his friend's body.

Hit in the chest, Nicholas fell backwards into the snow.

Rada's emotions took over. He raised his arms like Moses with the Ten Commandments and thrust his arms through the air as if throwing an invisible weight towards the assailant with the gun. The perpetrator bent beneath the tremendous weight of Rada's force. He was pushed into the snow deeper and deeper as the invisible weight continued to shove him into the soft whiteness. The force rendered him unable to move his arms and soon only his head appeared above the frozen tundra. He screamed into the emptiness as his head slowly disappeared below the whiteness. All that was left was the whistling of the wind above the ground where he had disappeared.

Rada ran to Nicholas and knelt next to him. The bullet had penetrated his heavy tundra jacket and entered into Nicholas' chest, very close to the heart. He quickly covered Nicholas with a blanket from one of the horses to protect him from the freezing elements. Rada held his hand over Nicholas' face and felt a faint breath coming from his mouth. Nicholas was alive, but barely.

Rada cradled Nicholas in his arms and began to cry. Suddenly he heard a sound above him and he looked up for its source. The woman on the horse had awakened and her eyes were just visible between the layers of her scarf, as she stared down at Rada. He was no longer alone.

She spoke from her perch, "Hey – get me down!!?" She wrestled with the ropes and nearly fell from the horse.

Rada replied in a panic, "No, No. I am very sorry. You are no longer a prisoner. We are here to rescue you now." He looked down at Nicholas and corrected himself. "Well, at least I am here to rescue you," he said sadly.

Rada stood up, leaving Nicholas unconscious in the snow, and released the woman from the horse. He untied her hands and helped her down.

"Thank you, and you are?" she said with a very proper Australian accent.

"I am Rada."

"Well Rada, it is certainly a pleasure to meet you. I was about to freeze my…my toes off," she said politely, with a bit more vigor than would be expected from a woman who had been tied to a horse in a blizzard. "I very much appreciate you taking a promenade through this particular park at this particular time."

"Park?" Rada looked at her questioningly.

"Okay, well no, not a park actually. That is just a line I am very fond of while making new friends on the tundra. But park or not, on occasion it is a wonderful place to promenade, unless of course, you happen to bump into renegades like this bunch."

He nodded and she continued, "My name is Cobie Dulan and if you haven't already surmised, I'm from Down Under."

Rada was puzzled, he did not connect with this woman. What was she talking about? He knew she was friendly, but could not piece together her meaning.

"Hey, weren't there four men?" she said looking in the direction of the fallen men.

He nodded again and said guiltily and somewhat embarrassed, "One man was too heavy for snow." He thought and continued, "He went down-under too."

"Hmm," she said pondering what that meant and then frowned at him suspiciously, "What about that man, is he your friend?"

Rada remembered now, and yelled, "Ah - yes, Nicholas! He has been shot. He is alive...I think."

They ran over to Nicholas and knelt beside him. Cobie pulled down the blanket and looked at his face for the first time. Nicholas didn't look very well. He was pale and breathing shallowly. Even so, she thought he was a very handsome man. Cobie quickly unzipped the tundra jacket, and pulled up his green shirt. There was a hole in his chest, oozing with blood. The green shirt had a large bloodied wet stain that covered the entire front of it.

"We're gonna need to take that bullet out and get him warm. Do you know if there is any shelter around here?"

Rada shook his head, and said, "I don't know. I am not from this part of the country."

"Hmm, well, that means we will have to find shelter on our own, unless those guys..." She looked back to where the three horsemen had been sprawled in the snow. They were gone. The rope that had tied them together lay in the snow; the rope had been burned in the middle. The men and all but one horse had completely disappeared.

"Well okay, there ya' go pardner Rada, it looks like it's you and me. And we better get moving ASAP and find some shelter. And I don't mean from this snow. Those guys came up from Skardu and they said something about a holy mission with more support on its way."

Rada looked around, "Where did they go?"

"It doesn't matter. We can't go to Skardu. We'll have to get your friend to a place where it is warmer and we can try to deal with his wound. We have to take care of your friend. Personally, I don't know if he can survive," said Cobie bluntly to Rada. "He's lost a lot of blood."

Rada forced words out, "Is there anything we can do?"

"I need to remove the bullet. You need to find a place to move him out of the snow."

Rada found a small cave against the foot of one of the mountains about a quarter mile away. It was more a divot than a cave, a deep scoop out of the rock, but it sufficed to provide cover from the snow and wind, and had an alcove off to the side in the back where they were totally isolated from the wind and the storm. They were hundreds of miles from civilization and from help. Cobie found a blanket in one of the packs on the remaining horse. She also grabbed the canvas sack, which she had previously been held prisoner inside.

Together they placed Nicholas on the blanket and pulled him into the shelter of the alcove at the back of the cave. Rada built a fire for warmth and light just outside the alcove where the smoke was sucked out into the blizzard's wind, but doom was in the air and his own regrets were close behind.

Why hadn't he been able to stop them? Why hadn't he seen that this might happen? How could he have stopped the bullet? These questions repeated themselves again and again in Rada's mind.

Cobie reached into the pocket of her parka and pulled out a Swiss Army knife. She removed the glove from her right hand and unfolded a tool like tweezers from the knife. Cobie placed the tweezers into the fire and poured some whiskey from her pack over them before she shoved the tips into the bullet hole in Nicholas' chest. He did not react at all, not a good sign. By the number of small bubbles in the blood, Cobie suspected the bullet might have pierced a lung. She dug deeper and extracted the bullet along with a piece of green shirt. She threw them into the snow. It was not as deep as she thought, but was lodged behind one of his ribs. The rib, she thought, might have been broken, piercing the lung. She tore long strips from the canvas sack and wrapped the strips around Nicholas' chest.

"Okay..." Cobie exhaled loudly, "I've removed the bullet and now we gotta keep him hydrated and warm."

Rada held Nicholas' hand and watched his chest heave with each gasping breath. He saw a flutter of Nicholas' eyelids in an apparent dream, or nightmare. He prayed, 'Nicholas can't die. He is the Magus. He has much to do.'

They both sat for a minute to re-group their emotions and accept their current situation.

Finally Cobie said, "So Rada, where are you from?" trying to get Rada back to reality, or at least, to get his mind off Nicholas.

Rada looked at her. He was tired, dazed, and very worried about Nicholas, but he realized she was trying to make conversation and show support.

"Oh I ... oh ... I am from the mountains." He paused. "I live at a monastery."

"Are you a monk?"

"No ... I am an apprentice, a novice. Not yet monk."

"What is your Order?"

"Order?"

"Your religion? Are you Christian?"

"Oh ... no ... I did not understand. We practice a type of ancient Zoroastrianism," said Rada with a sense of pride.

"Hmm, okay. I am not even sure I can say that. Well, that's one religion I don't know much about. But good for you. We could use a little faith right now. So if you know some good prayers, now would be a perfect time to throw in a good word to your higher power."

Rada nodded and closed his eyes briefly.

135

She continued, "So how did you come to be here? And who is he?" She looked at Nicholas.

Rada followed her glance but continued with the polite conversation, "We were coming down from the mountain. He was going home. He is from the United States. Do you know where that is?"

"Yes silly, of course I know where that is," she replied.

"What do you do, Miss Cobie? Why are you here? You do not sound like you are from here, either."

"No chap, I'm not from here," her accent was very pronounced. "I'm from Australia. Canberra, Australia to be exact. I'm a professor at the Australian National University."

"Ah... so you are a teacher like Nicholas. I am still a student."

"I believe we are all students. I may be a teacher of Geology. I teach what I know and I know a little more than the average person. You, on the other hand, know more than I about your religion, the Z-faith or whatever it is, and most likely more about these particular mountains. So in that sense, you too, are a teacher for me. We are all students, continuing to learn."

"Yes, I agree. We are all students. Nicholas is actually also a student of my faith, but he is a teacher, too. He is student of many things," said Rada with his melancholy emotions returning. The tears started down his cheeks, but he continued, forgetting where he had left off with his questions, "Why are you here?"

She too watched Nicholas labor for breath, and answered, "I am here because I am a geologist. This is one of the world's most geologically active areas between two colliding continents. These ranges may have caused climate change when they were formed over forty million years ago and caused the global climate to cool, triggering an ice age. They were important in the past, they are important to study for the future. I have been studying infrared satellite photos that show there may be many more hidden caverns and 'hot zones' than may have been previously discovered."

"And, besides, I love the feel of the granite beneath my feet. It helps me put things in proper perspective, sometimes taking me where few have gone before. There is an Italian legend and according to their ancient myth, Rock was known as Scylla, personified as a female monster. I like to believe this creature Scylla waits for me in every molecule of stone and in the vastness of the open mountain range; for I am the one who has tamed the monster and understands its very soul." She paused, and realized she had stepped behind her podium. She looked up from Nicholas and saw Rada staring at her.

"Truthfully, I just love rocks and hiking."

"Have you been here before?" he asked.

"No, never here. I have been all over the world, flown to some of the most remote places on the planet. Namadgi National Park was my headquarters for a while. But, I finally managed to get a year off to explore. Throughout my life, this mountain range has drawn me, beckoned me. There is an intense feeling being here, like I am destined to discover some new secret in these mountains. This year in particular, the mountains seemed to call my very soul."

"There are many secrets in these mountains," responded Rada knowingly. "They are vast. Who knows what truly lies hidden in every crack and crevice?"

"Exactly. That's why I'm here. I want to find out what secrets are hidden in the rocks and the crevices," she said smiling confidently.

"All of the mountain's secrets may not just be in its rocks and crevices but in the minds of those seeking the secrets," said Rada with some knowledge.

She looked at him trying deeply to understand who he might be.

"Why were you tied to the horse?" continued Rada.

"Well, there I was having a peaceful meal around a cozy fire when those nice men raced through my camp, destroyed my tent and threw my gear all over the place. I've had to deal with all sorts of people and nasty situations in my day, but disregard for science is ignorance at its worst."

"How did you get tied to the horse?"

"I think they wanted me for later."

"Weren't you afraid?"

"Yes and no. I am a rather self-reliant woman, and I was pretty confident that I would be able to get to my satellite phone at some point. Not that I don't appreciate you showing up when you did."

"You're welcome," responded Rada who was very impressed with this woman's resilience and demeanor. "So, what we can do for Nicholas?"

Chapter 21

*We are somewhat more than ourselves in our
sleeps, and the slumber of the body seems to be
but the waking of the soul.*

Sir Thomas Browne

The two days break from Mount Weather was a welcomed event for Jen. August in D.C. was wonderful. The sun was shining and it was beginning to feel like fall was just around the corner. Jen had forgotten how great it was to walk in the sunshine and feel a breeze after spending so much time underground. She had actually gotten used to the darkness of Mount Weather, and the artificial fluorescent lighting. These two days off also coincided with Sansa and Tori's return from their tour in Japan. It sounded like they had a very successful and well-received tour, which was to be expected, they were excellent performers. But they still were very glad to be home again.

Jen's nightmares still continued; the same split second images of things she didn't understand and words from some language that she didn't know. She tried to remember the words but she was not able to pull them from her mind.

Jen, Sansa, and Tori were all worried about Nicholas. No one had heard anything from him, no postcard, no call, nothing. It was very unusual for Nicholas. Sansa wondered if Nicholas was trying to reach Jen through her dreams. Maybe these were the images and words she was seeing. Jen doubted his reasoning and said she thought it might have something more to do with an experiment they were performing at work.

Sansa was what was known in the magical community as a mentalist on stage, practicing mind-reading, using magic tricks which did indeed allow him, in a sense, to read people's minds and body language. He was a big skeptic in the world of mediums and psychics and did his best, while not on the road, to de-bunk the fakes. While performing, he never claimed to be a psychic. He said that he had only honed his mind through mental exercises and that he had learned to use the senses that everyone else already possessed. He had trained himself to recognize small flutters in eye movements, changes in facial expressions or perspiration and other almost imperceptible signs. He could read other people's thoughts by his own enhanced abilities and of course, a few magic tricks as well.

Although he was skeptical of self-proclaimed mediums and psychics, he was still a firm believer in the connectivity between the minds of people, and of the infinite possibilities of the mind. He was a licensed hypnotist and was continually amazed at what could be accomplished and discovered while a person was hypnotized.

Perhaps hypnotism would reveal more of what Jen had seen in her mind's eye. Sansa thought she might be able to recall the words she saw and write them down. Jen had initially resisted the idea of hypnotism, but finally agreed. Her hesitation was only because she would have to report it to the security office at Mt. Weather. There was always a fear by government security that under hypnosis some secret might be verbalized, which would otherwise be held back by the conscious mind.

Sansa chose to hypnotize Jen in his garage studio. It was sound-proofed and the only noise that could be heard was from a fountain, as water trickled down rocks into a small pool. Sansa had Jen lie down on a comfortable sofa and close her eyes. Then he spoke to her softly, calmly, and hypnotically. Jen was very easy to hypnotize.

A yellow legal pad and pen were close to Jen on a table by the sofa. With free association, Jen timidly wrote the phrase on the pad: Coraxo cahisa coremepe, od belanusa Lucala azodiazodore paebe Soba. She was agitated about something deeper in her subconscious beneath the words she was writing. Sansa worked to calm her and woke her as soon as she put the pen down. They both

looked at what she had written. It wasn't Latin. It wasn't a language either one of them could identify. It made no sense.

Jen was even more terrified. Why was she receiving a foreign language phrase from Burton? What was he trying to communicate to her? Why had the phrase made her feel so poorly? The images gave her such terrible nightmares and left her feeling desolate, angry, and hopeless. Could it be that Nicholas was trying to reach her from wherever he was and that this had nothing to do with Burton? But why wouldn't Nicholas have sent her something she understood? There were only questions and more questions and no answers.

Sansa said he knew a linguist and asked Jen if he could take the phrase to his friend at the University in Georgetown. Jen agreed, although she knew this might be a breach in security. In her soul, she knew there was something wrong, and the least of her problems was a breach in security.

*   *   *

Sansa introduced Jen to a distinguished, grey-haired woman at the University. Anxious to know what the phrase meant, Jen handed Professor Fogerty the yellow paper where she had written the odd phrase.

"Well, I can't tell you what it is, but I can tell you what it isn't. It isn't Greek, Latin, Spanish, Italian or Portuguese, but seems to stem from a pre-Latin based language. It may be a primitive language from long ago that I have not studied. It may even be a code. Sorry I can't be of more help to you, but let me hold onto this and see what I can come up with." Professor Fogerty was sympathetic and could sense Jen's discomfort and need for urgent answers.

That night, Jen suffered more nightmares. She tossed and turned, waking herself up in a sweat with screaming. Sansa and Tori rushed into Jen's bedroom. They were very concerned.

"Should we take you to the hospital? Are you okay?" Tori was at a loss to know what to do for Jen.

"No, no, I am okay – just a cup of tea maybe?"

"I have some chamomile... That might help to calm you." Tori left to make the tea. Sansa held Jen's hand.

"Was it the words again?"

"Yes – it's not knowing what they mean and who they are coming from." Jen sat upright in the bed and pulled the covers up to her chin. "I feel like something awful is happening and I don't know what, where, or why. It's a totally helpless feeling that I just can't seem to shake."

"It doesn't help that we still have not heard from Nicholas."

"No – his cell's still not registering anything at all. Do you think he's trying to contact me?" Jen asked.

"I wish I knew, Jen. I wish I knew."

Chapter 22

*We call it death to leave this world, but were we
once out of it, and enstated into the happiness of
the next, we should think it were dying indeed to
come back to it again.*

Thomas Sherlock

There was no pain, only suffering. The struggle was for
each breath of air, like a prisoner grasping for a key out of reach.
Oxygen didn't seem sufficient anymore. The breaths were shallow,
the reward minimal. Nicholas realized the struggle was nearly over.
The solitude to contemplate the oneness of being was a moment
away. His gasps began to reach harder into the ether but were
becoming further apart.

The world around him was quiet and peaceful. One more
reach for that last molecule of air, that last breath of life, and he
would be done. His body stopped its motion, his soul could move
on. The struggle was over, and the silence was complete now. Peace
at last.

Light appeared, foggy and hazy. Slowly his vision cleared
as he began to feel the weight of his body dissipating. Nicholas
became weightless and began to rise out of his earthly body. He
looked down on the scene below. He saw the flickering fire dancing
more brightly than any fire he had ever seen. He saw Rada and the
woman who'd been tied to the horse. Their bodies glowed with an
aura of existence beyond their physicality. He saw his own body.
There was no glow; it was an empty shell of lifeless matter.

Rada was bowed over Nicholas' body while Cobie had
turned away. Nicholas experienced a deep sense of peace and
contentment and was prepared to move on. He could not hear
Rada's whimpers or the crackle of the fire, but he heard a voice in a
wind-like tone. It was a voice he recognized.

"Remember who you are... Remember the world... Remember your responsibilities... Remember the magic... Remember... To... Be..."

And he did remember. He looked at Rada and Cobie and remembered everything. The contentment in his leaving was gone in an instant. There was no fear either, only focus. He must get back. He must get back inside his body. He must continue his training, he must save ... save ... the ...

'Save the what?' he thought. 'Why did he have that thought?'

But it didn't matter. He began moving toward his body as the ball had moved around his body at the Cloister. He floated toward it and willfully morphed his soul into every molecule within the dead form. Rada placed his hand on Nicholas' chest. It felt warm and grew hotter. With a jolt Nicholas' consciousness bolted from the surreal to the real, and the pain within his body returned in a flash as he gasped for air.

Nicholas yelled aloud, "AAHHHH!"

Eyes open, he raised his head and stared at Rada and the woman in wonder. They could only stare back in shock.

He dropped his head back to the floor of the shallow cave and stared up at the ceiling. Every cell had been revived from death to life; it was like an electrical shock wave throughout all of his bodily matter. The pain was bothersome, but not as bad as when he first returned a moment ago. He could feel again, and feeling all, was not bad.

"You are alive," said Rada.

"Yes, Rada. I am alive."

"You must rest," said the woman. "You have been through too much and we don't want to lose you."

"Who are you?" asked Nicholas.

"Cobie. She's from 'Down Under'" said Rada emphatically.

"I do feel much better. Besides a little pain in my back, I feel a lot better now."

"Don't fool yourself," said Cobie, "You're still in pretty nasty shape here and ..."

Nicholas grabbed her hand with his left hand and placed his right hand over his chest. He squeezed her hand and the air between his right hand and torso became blurry and distorted, as though a heat-mirage had formed between them. Cobie tried to pull her hand away but, to her surprise, Nicholas held it tightly. She heard and even felt an unexplained hum as the wound began closing in his chest and his body began to heal. Cobie's energy was synergistically promoting the healing of his body.

In a moment it was done. He released her hand and the healing heat-mirage faded. Cobie withdrew her hand. It felt warm, almost hot.

"I feel used!" she laughed nervously.

Rada and Cobie backed off in amazement. Rada was smiling. Cobie was not. She was scared and weakened from the exchange of energy.

"You see, I do feel much better now," said Nicholas as he threw the blanket aside and jumped to his feet. "Much better."

"Let me see!" said Cobie rather forcefully, and with a touch of fear.

Nicholas lifted up his garments showing the wrapped wound. Cobie unwrapped the canvas cloth. There was no longer a bullet hole, only a small reddened, irritated area on his skin.

"How'd you do that?" she asked now in amazement.

"Magic," he replied with confidence.

"Magic? How?" Cobie insisted.

"A magician never reveals his secrets." Nicholas smiled.

"Alright, well who the hell are you guys? That was no magic that I am aware of!" she said backing away.

Nicholas looked deep into her eyes, "Listen. I am a quantum physicist, and there are a lot more possibilities in this universe than there are magical secrets. Let it go at that for now. We have much more to worry about, like getting out of here."

Cobie calmed down a bit but only because she realized she had no choice. 'Where else could she turn at this point?'

So Cobie turned her thoughts to the possibility of the horsemen returning. She withdrew a well-worn map of the mountain range from the cleavage between her ample breasts, unfolded the map and smoothed out the wrinkled paper.

"Okay, I will let it go for now, but just until we get somewhere safe. So you think you can travel?" she said with a sudden realization of hope.

Nicholas nodded.

"Well, we have to stay away from Skardu," she pointed to the map. Since the rogue warriors had apparently come from Skardu, Rada, Nicholas and Cobie agreed to leave via another route.

"We could cross to India here…" she pointed to the Siachen Glacier. "That would bring us to Ghyari where I have stored supplies for my expedition."

"Expedition?" Nicholas was unaware of her situation.

"Yes, I have been on a geological expedition, but I can tell you that as we travel. We need to get going now."

Nicholas shivered. "Cross a glacier?" Going this route did mean they would have to travel across the Siachen Glacier, the largest alpine glacier on earth with nearly two trillion cubic feet of ice. It wouldn't be an easy trek.

"How is Ghyari safer? The Pakistani and Indian armies have been battling over that land for nearly twenty years. How will we get through?" Nicholas was not convinced this was the best choice.

"It won't be easy, but I know the way." This was the route that Cobie had originally planned to take before she'd been captured. Reaching her supplies at the base in Ghyari would allow her to proceed with her plans and Nicholas and Rada could buy staples to finish their trek. It was, in her mind, the best choice.

Rada nodded in agreement. He felt her confidence.

"So be it," said Nicholas, feeling it as well.

Unfortunately, this route did take them to the world's highest battleground in the continued dispute over Kashmir. However, the evil force they felt from the marauders seemed worse than the unknown evils of the war. Cobie also felt confident that she had an 'in' with the Pakistani army who would consider them independents, or neutrals, as far as the war was concerned. She had already coordinated her own stay on their base.

As the group, horse and yaks walked southwest the sky was a deep blue at its zenith, and like a prism, evolving to indigo and eventually to black. The cold night air could stop the flow of blood in its path, but they had to press on. It was important for them to reach a safe place.

Nicholas immersed himself in thought as they traversed the frozen tundra. His wound felt completely healed, but his head was still not focused. He had many voices and memories in his head that he could not seem to pin down. First and foremost, who were those marauders, and how did Cobie fit into the picture, either with them or as a captive or just being here alone in the mountains? He had died, he knew that, and had somehow managed to get back into his physical being and heal himself. These were not lessons he had learned at the Cloister, yet it felt perfectly natural and instinctive for him to heal himself using the life force from within Cobie. He had plenty to think about as they traveled and not a lot of answers.

*   *   *

When they finally arrived at Ghyari, the base commander was expecting them. Cobie had contacted the commander by satellite phone to coordinate the needed supplies for her expedition, and also to let the commander know she was bringing two companions. After some initial questioning as to the origin of her companions, the commander concluded they were not from the Indian army, and escorted them to their quarters.

Rada, Cobie and Nicholas sat in a sparse stone-walled barrack, with one desk and three cots. A wood-burning stove occupied the middle of the room and they huddled around the heat, sharing tales of origin and history.

"So, you're an astronomer?" asked Cobie of Nicholas.

"Yes, I am both an astronomer and astrophysicist."

"And for my own edification, you are in the mountains why?" asked Cobie.

"Ooooooh, a very long story, and I'm sure we don't need to go into that here and now. Let's just say I came to study in a mountain monastery with Rada here."

Cobie looked at them both, and knew there was much more to be said. She was very intrigued. She liked this professor of astronomy. He was intriguing, mysterious, smart, handsome, and had a little something else. Some aura of knowledge or power… She wasn't sure, but what he did in the mountains to heal himself obviously was not something the average astronomy professor, quantum physicist, or anyone else, was capable of doing.

"And what about your situation, Dr. Dulan? Who were your wonderful companions? The ones who had you tied to a horse?" asked Nicholas.

"Truthfully, I don't know. Renegades, military deserters, who knows?" responded Cobie.

148

"I know," said Rada while stirring the coals in the stove with an iron rod.

Cobie and Nicholas looked at him, surprised. When Rada continued to focus on the fire without speaking Nicholas prompted, "You know?"

"Yes... those evil men were sent by the Others to kill you, Dr. Thompson," he paused.

Nicholas asked, "By others? What others?"

"Where there is good, there is bad. It is the balance of the universe," said Rada.

"I understand that Rada, but who are these Others? If they are trying to kill me, I sure as hell would like to know more about them," said Nicholas, perturbed.

"The good news is the few that are near are not as advanced as you or I in the ways of the Magi. We have a big advantage."

"Great. Now can you please tell me who they are and just what we are dealing with? I must know my enemy, always." Nicholas was getting exasperated with Rada's explanation. 'Why was he withholding information?' he thought to himself.

"Soon Tenzin will contact you and tell you what you need to know."

"Well, gee, that takes a load off my mind," responded Nicholas sarcastically. Nicholas looked to Cobie and shook his head.

*   *   *

The trio rested in Ghyari overnight and the next morning obtained the supplies they needed to continue. They had decided to leave the horse and keep only the yaks for the rest of their trek. Cobie agreed to stay with Nicholas and Rada on their journey. They all felt she would be safer staying with them until they could distance themselves from their attackers. And she was beginning to get a warm, nice feeling inside that she had not felt for a long time in regards to Nicholas. She felt he was very special. She thought perhaps she would travel as far as New Delhi and then catch a plane back home. Perhaps.

They decided to present the horse to the Pakistani army as a gift for their lodging. Good karma never hurt anyone, and who knew if they might have to pass this way again? After breakfast, they began their journey towards India to the east to escape all conflicts; Pakistani, Indian, and Magi, or at least that was the plan.

Over the next week they traveled by day, and camped at night. The days were mostly bright and clear, while the nights were riddled with jewels of stellar light. They crossed the Saltori Ridge and the Nubra River on their journey towards the village of Leh, a major town in the north of India. It had originally been known as the capital of the Himalayan kingdom of Ladakh, but was now known as the Leh District in the state of Jammu and Kashmir, India. The dominant structure in the village was the now-derelict Royal Palace, whose stone walls rose from a craggy stone hill overlooking the city at an altitude of almost twelve thousand feet.

Built by King Sengge Namgyal in the 17th century, Leh Palace was later abandoned when Kashmiri forces besieged it in the mid-19th century. Nine stories high, the upper floors had accommodated the royal family while the stables and storerooms were located in the lower levels.

The cobble-stoned street in the village wound around colorful two and three-storied Ladakh houses that were adorned with brightly painted windows overlooking little gardens with blossoming cosmos, poppies and hollyhocks. Everywhere there were men villagers and clusters of little children with sunburnt rosy cheeks and sparkling eyes who would greet them with the all-encompassing *jule* (hello, goodbye, thank-you and please). There were no women in the streets and Cobie felt self-conscious. Rada and Nicholas, however, felt welcomed and comforted to see some type of civilization again.

The village was dotted with prayer wheels. The locals would turn the symbolic wheel as they watched the travelers pass. It was the roulette wheel of the Gods, where it lands, nobody knows...or do they?

A network of narrow canals lined with wild irises channeled the river water to all parts of the village. There was a constant, gurgling sound of flowing water as the three of them trekked along the cobble-stoned streets. Higher up the mountain, above Leh Palace, was the Namgyal Tsemo Gompa monastery, the travelers' objective. The enigmatic, stark structure loomed over the town. The Namgyal rulers had built it in 1430. In contrast to its stark exterior, the inside walls of the monastery were covered with beautiful frescos and finely painted Buddhist scriptures. A massive three-story gold statue of the Maitrieya Buddha, the future Buddha, sat in the entrance hall surrounded by other ancient sculptures. Rada had known about the monastery in Leh. He had told his companions of a monk living there who had visited the Cloister of the Magi in the past. There was a casual relationship between the monks of Leh and the monks of the Cloister. The three travelers had decided to take advantage of this relationship since finding a trusting host and a safe haven seemed to be of utmost importance. Nicholas and Rada realized this more so than Cobie.

However, Cobie too, was beginning to piece together enough knowledge about the Cloister of the Magi and her companions during her week long journey to realize that she was embarking on the very journey for which she had been longing, and had actually searched, her entire life. As a scientist, she wanted to know all. And there was a lot more going on here on these travels than she had any scientific answers for. Satisfying her professional curiosity was her number one drive, or perhaps her number two drive, but very high on her list.

Rada, Nicholas, and Cobie found the monastery easily by following the footpaths up to the Palace and then beyond. Once the trio reached the monastery, they found the monk who had visited the Cloister. They told him in secrecy what they thought he should know of their journey. He listened intently and politely nodded. He understood their need for temporary sanctuary.

"I, too, have sought sanctuary in times of need," he said. He told them he would make arrangements for them to stay as long as they liked. He was indebted to the Magi at the Cloister for several visits of his own in the past.

They explained that they intended to travel to New Delhi as soon as possible, and from there, they hoped to find passage to America. Truthfully, they would have liked to stay longer at the monastery to recuperate, but they feared intervention from the marauders, or 'the Others' as Rada called them.

They decided the best mode of travel would be to hitch a ride on a truck to Manali and then take a bus to Delhi. The trucks traveling the trade route could not be traced, so if they could get to Manali undetected it would then be safe enough to use the public transportation system.

The following morning, Nicholas meditated at the monastery while Cobie dressed as one of the local women in the village and properly hid her face so as not to stand out as an outsider and then she and Rada searched the town for trucks running goods back and forth to Delhi. They acquired "space" on a truck with a driver from the local truck park for five hundred rupees, half the price they had bartered for the yaks earlier in the day. The vehicle was a ten-ton cargo truck that showed signs of much use. The back was enclosed by a large canvas tarp stretched over metal ribbing. The driver was not against making frequent stops to pick up other passengers and their baggage along the way. Oftentimes the baggage had four legs and used the truck as their personal lavatory. There were no seats and the canvas sides prevented them from seeing any of the land they were passing through. Rada, Nicholas and Cobie made the uncomfortable four-hundred-ninety kilometer journey to Manali in two days and then very gratefully took a bus to Delhi without incident.

Delhi was where ancient and modern India collided with startling results. Many tourists stayed in hotels with modern conveniences only to step outside the lobby to see lawns being cut by an antique piece of machinery pulled by a bullock. Officially, there were two separate cities; the old city of Delhi and New Delhi. New Delhi was largely built by the British and had clean, modern, tree-lined streets. Old Delhi was considerably less manicured and less clean but with famous architecture dating back to the 10th century. It was this juxtaposition of worlds that made Delhi such a fascinating city.

All the major hotels had richly decorated bars, aiming for either a British Raj or a plush Continental look. The threesome had opted to stay in the old part of Delhi, hoping that would keep them below the radar. Rada entered what appeared to be a house that had been converted to a restaurant and motioned for Nicholas and Cobie to join him.

The father of the family that owned the restaurant greeted the guests. Children were serving other patrons while the mother, dressed in a linen burka that covered her entire face, cooked in the kitchen. All the occupants of the restaurant were men who wore robes and turbans and eyed the Occidental newcomers suspiciously.

The walls were decorated with Moslem framed art, typical Indian fabrics and bright colors. The father brought the trio into a room that was perhaps a small bedroom before. There were four small tables, each surrounded by four chairs. One other table was occupied with several Indian men who watched and listened overtly to the trio.

Rada ordered for Nicholas and Cobie. When the food appeared on the table, it looked delicious; flat breads, sliced cucumbers, stews with roasted vegetables that were absolutely scrumptious. Having eaten the Cloister food for three months and dried meat, fruits and nuts on the journey down from the Karakorum Mountains, Nicholas was ravenous. He ate for two, leaving nothing on the serving platters. Cobie, too, had kept up with Nicholas, thoroughly enjoying the food.

"I know I'm going to regret eating so much but this was sooooo good!" exclaimed Nicholas, leaning back in his chair and patting his stomach. Rada handed him a cup of tea.

"This will help you digest all you have eaten." The green tea would absorb the grease from the foods and in doing so, would eliminate the stuffed feeling.

Rada motioned for the owner to come to the table. "I want to introduce you to my friends, Cobie and Nicholas. He is a magician."

Nicholas realized that he must sing for his supper and rose to the occasion. He stood and held out his hands in front of him, materializing four large coins in his left hand. One by one he made the coins disappear from the left and appear in his right until all four coins were in his right hand. Then, one by one, he made them totally disappear into the air. He pulled a coin from behind the ear of the host, from Rada's jacket lapel, and from beneath Cobie's hand resting on her knee. Other guests started coming into the room to watch. Nicholas pulled another coin from the tray of one of the host's children, and another from the air and placed them all into a glass on the table. After a barrage of coins appeared, Nicholas dumped them into the glass, nodded to the host, picked up the glass and handed it to him for his tip.

Cobie was absolutely amazed. It was her very first time watching Nicholas perform and she was delighted. He was quite an entertainer. He knew exactly when to milk the air, the audience, and fool them all. She clapped and giggled like a little girl watching her first magic show.

After dinner, the three travelers decided they deserved a little more ambience and quiet to continue their discussions. They traveled by taxi to the Taj for a nightcap before retiring and beginning the next stage of their journey to America. Although the Taj Hotel was known for its plush and excessively expensive five-star ambience, the trio just wanted a drink and a safe place to relax. For the first time, after all their adventures, they were finally warm and felt they could talk openly.

"I want to know how you did it." Cobie took a long sip of wine and leaned back, searching Nicholas' face.

"Are you a serious magician? Do you want to perform such feats of magic yourself?" inquired Nicholas.

"No – but I want to know how you did it… I can't stand not knowing."

"It takes lots of practice, hours and hours with coins – and shows I have no life." Nicholas smiled again.

"No – I'm talking about your recovery… How did you heal so quickly? What magic did you use to instantaneously repair the bullet hole? I've never seen anything like it." Cobie had been trying to pry into Nicholas' special abilities for weeks now. She was totally perplexed and the wine was encouraging her curiosity. She leaned forward and touched his hand.

Electricity raced through both of them. Nicholas started to pull his hand away, slightly startled at her touch but left his hand on the table, wondering what would ensue.

"I knew you were dead. I took the bullet out of your chest and then after we moved you to the rock shelter, I saw your breathing stop. You died!" She shook her head in disbelief. She looked to Rada. "You saw that, too! I know you thought he was dead. How did you do it???"

Nicholas shrugged, "Some things are better left unexplained."

"What will it take for you to reveal your secret to me?" Cobie's coyness could not be missed. "Just what did you learn in that Cloister?"

Nicholas looked at Rada for support. Rada was busy looking at the soda gun behind the bar and drinking the virgin fruit drink with a brightly colored umbrella that had arrived in front of him. He really couldn't figure out how those different colored liquids came out of one receptacle. He had not been paying attention to the conversation, or so it seemed. His senses were definitely on overload.

Nicholas smiled back at her, about to begin to explain about the Cloister when Rada finally spoke up, "Time to go!" as he gulped down the rest of his fruity drink. He tucked the umbrella in his pocket.

*   *   *

On the streets, the threesome walked with their backpack gear among the camels, mules and robed city dwellers. Cobie located a large, older, but well maintained building with a Roman arch and entered. Ornately decorated in earth-toned colors, the hotel had a very friendly and inviting atmosphere, in spite of what appeared to be bullet holes in the exterior walls.

Cobie secured a suite with two bedrooms and a living room area, the largest accommodations the modest hotel could offer for the other half of the yak money. Neither Cobie nor Nicholas were comfortable yet using credit cards while they were in a country where there might be 'Others' waiting for them to reveal themselves. The city noises could be heard from the street below their hotel room, but Rada, Nicholas and Cobie were so tired they heard nothing.

"I'm exhausted!" Nicholas announced as he threw his backpack on the floor.

"We're all exhausted, but I need to ask you something, Dr. Thompson," said Cobie.

"Okay," he replied looking deep into her eyes.

"Just out of curiosity, what's your plan now? Where do you go from here?" she asked coyly, sensing he really hadn't thought it through yet.

"Yeah... well, okay... there's an interesting question. Truthfully, I'm not sure." He looked at Rada and continued.

"The plan was for Rada and me to reach the United States. I was going to get him a student visa to study at the university."

"Does Rada have suitable identification to accomplish this task?" she asked knowing that he probably did not.

"No, he doesn't. I planned to deal with that before our flight to the States. But it will probably prove to be a little more difficult now that our whereabouts are being scrutinized," he replied.

"Well, I have a few connections in New Delhi that may be of some help, that is, if you are willing to consider my proposal."

"Proposal?"

"Yes. I had been planning a trip to the United States later this year. Actually, I wanted to go to Yosemite National Park to do some studies on the granite formations, but based on your connection with the University, and my curiosity about you two, I think I'd like to join you on your voyage. It accelerates my plans by a couple months, months I would have been on the Pakistani tundra if I had not been so rudely interrupted. But I'd like to go with you to America."

Nicholas felt conflicted. He enjoyed getting to know Cobie over the last weeks; he was actually not looking forward to saying goodbye. But, he feared for her safety.

"You hardly know us and it could be dangerous, based on the recent events in the mountains. I'm not sure what risks may be involved."

"I'm prepared to take any risk. Besides, without my help, I suspect getting Rada to America may be a bit more of a challenge than you are prepared to tackle."

"Well, I don't know... I really don't." Nicholas replied honestly. "I guess I can't stop a determined woman who's already made up her mind, huh?"

"Right you are," she answered. "So we have a deal?"

"Deal," he said with mixed feelings of regret and relief. It would be great to have the help with passports and IDs for Rada. Cobie had been a good traveling companion so far, and another comrade wasn't such a bad idea.

"But we do need to get to the States as soon as possible." He paused, and looked at her seriously, "I think there may be some dire issues that I need to deal with."

"You sense a disturbance in the force Luke?" she said half teasingly.

"Yeah I'm sorry, but it is something like that. It's just these 'Others' and... a feeling I have," he said solemnly.

"No problem, let me make a few phone calls and I'll bet we can be on a plane by tomorrow," she said in an attempt to raise his spirits.

"Plane!" said Rada with an inkling of fear and excitement.

"It's hard to believe this time tomorrow, we'll be on our way to Los Angeles," mused Cobie, smiling at Nicholas.

Rada yawned and headed to one of the bedrooms. "Nicholas, Tenzin will be contacting you tonight. Prepare to write. It will be a history lesson. I must go and practice the Grand Silence before bed. My head is spinning." He retired, promising to meet with them early in the morning.

Cobie slumped into the small couch. "I'll sleep here!"

"Oh no – you get the other bedroom. That's for me!" argued Nicholas.

"Yeah, so you can wake up like a pretzel tomorrow and complain all day, no thanks..." She smiled. Nicholas sat beside her on the couch, and he stared into her eyes.

"I feel like I've known you for years... not just a few weeks."

"I'm not sure if that's good or bad," she replied, secretly pleased he felt the same way she was feeling.

And then as abruptly as he had sat down, Nicholas got up and paced.

"You okay?" Cobie was perplexed. Everything had seemed to be going in the right direction... now he was pulling away.

"Yeah – I've... well, I've avoided relationships for a long, long time now and I'm a little rusty."

Cobie laughed out loud. "You don't seem the type! I'm sure you have many women back home. Ah – that's it... You don't know what to do with me back home."

"No, no, no – that's not it at all," said Nicholas staring at the floor.

Cobie was puzzled.

Nicholas sat back down beside her, "Yeah sure, I used to have lots of girlfriends. That was the easy part. Everyone loves an entertainer, especially a magician. Not the astrophysicist as much, by the way. And I was even married. To a girl named Amy," as he said her name he felt a twinge of emotional pain.

"She was my soul mate so to speak. I know it sounds silly, but I believe in a much deeper relationship between beings, as well as particles. Before Amy, I'd enjoy a girl's company but it was just as easy to be without them and practice magic. I got to the point that I felt I was using women... When Mom and Dad died, Amy was in the plane, too."

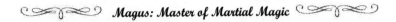

It was hard for him to say that she had actually died.

"I had my sister to take care of. It was easy not to think about having a relationship. It left more time for other things, for practice, for study ..."

Nicholas gently moved a lock of hair that had fallen across her forehead. He hadn't touched her since the bar and this touch was just as startling. It was like the static electricity that followed the heat of your hand; a warmth, a glow that reached deep inside. It was as though both of their energies were searching and connecting to one another. He knew she had felt it, too.

He thought, 'Was this the right thing to do? Did he really want to break the three-year relationship fast? Did he want to start a relationship with someone who would leave him? Or might die? And did Amy even die?' This was too much to think about.

Cobie read his mind, "This isn't the time..." She gently touched his cheek with the back of her hand, got up and went into the bedroom, shyly closing the door. She leaned against the closed door for a second before slowly walking across the room and pulling back the covers of the bed with a 'sigh'.

Chapter 23

> *It is not the eye that sees the beauty of the*
> *heaven, nor the ear that hears the sweetness of*
> *music or glad tidings of prosperous occurrence,*
> *but the SOUL, that perceives all the relishes of*
> *sensual and intellectual perfections; and the*
> *more noble and excellent the soul is, the greater*
> *and more savory are its perceptions.*

Jeremy Taylor

Nicholas sat in the hotel room at the small table provided for the occasional business traveler. He had his Magi notebook open and was prepared to write. His mind was calm but he had many questions and even more concerns. The room was dark except for the reading lamp above his notebook. He closed his eyes and leaned back in the chair. He concentrated on his breathing and the silence beyond.

"*I understand you have had an encounter with the Others,*" said Tenzin.

Nicholas was not surprised to hear her gentle voice. He answered calmly as if the voice had been expected at the precise moment he had heard it.

"Yes," said Nicholas solemnly. He was humbled to be speaking again with Tenzin. He believed he truly understood the goodness and the honor within the being, and within the Magi. He was honored to be a disciple.

"*It is unfortunate, but we are glad that Rada was there to assist. He will be a good companion as you go forth in your world.*"

Nicholas nodded silently.

"*It is good that you have recovered fully from your wound. Rada tells me you nearly died.*"

161

"Yes, this is true, but I heard a voice calling me back ... was that you?"

"No, it was not my voice you heard."

"I also discovered some powers from within I was not taught at the cloister. Like the power to heal using the energy and life force of another."

They paused to consider this for a moment and then Tenzin continued, *"For now, we should appreciate you are alive. You will continue to grow on your own even while you are away from the cloister. You have a strong foundation. But for now, we need to move on. Unfortunately, we do not have a millennium to re-construct the complete story of the Others whom you encountered, and their relationship with the Magi. I will have to give you a brief history to reveal the origins of the conflict, and bring you to our current position."*

Nicholas thought to himself knowing that Tenzin would hear his thoughts, 'I would very much appreciate any enlightenment you can provide.'

"Thousands of years ago, our society thrived on another world where life flowed in abundance. There were great rivers, mountains, lush meadows, a vast variety of animals and vegetation as well as intelligent life. But true intelligence is not necessarily quantitative. As it is in any confined social environment, there were those who sought knowledge and peace, and there were those who sought knowledge and power."

"Those who sought peace were known as the Magi and those who, in the end, sought power over all, were known as the Daemons."

"The Daemons created a multitude of machines that gradually destroyed the natural resources on the planet. Their machines were built to increase the productivity of other machines, which increased their wealth and power. The Magi were well aware of the fine thread that was being broken. This thread held together the symbiotic relationship between intelligent life and the planet itself. But the Daemons were not convinced. They wanted more; more machines to assist in their production, and more power over all, including the Magi. They wanted power and authority over the planet itself ..."

"*In the end, we fled. We had become a liability for the Daemons, and we were the next to be sacrificed. We fled and found a new home here, on your planet. We intermingled with your race and started a new colony. After many years, we eventually settled in the mountains at the Cloister, where we have resided in peace and harmony for over two thousand years.*"

Nicholas didn't write any of this down. He sat with his eyes closed; his head back and listened to the tale.

"*The Daemons continued to ravage the planet after we had fled and eventually, as we had predicted, the natural environment changed dramatically causing the atmosphere of the planet to dissipate. There was no time for the Daemons to escape. They had dug tunnels and built underground fortresses lest they needed to protect themselves from enemy threats. Ironically, they needed these underground resources to protect themselves from the enemy they themselves had created, the environment. The atmosphere had dissipated and they had nowhere to turn. In the end, they had to abandon the surface and move underground where they exist to this present day.*"

Tenzin paused at length, and the single candle on Nicholas' table flickered.

"*Their thirst for power was not quenched. They continued to manipulate others, even at great distances, from their underground abodes. They, to this day, have ignorant followers working their dark magic above ground on this planet. I say ignorant because if these followers truly understood the new objective of the Daemons, they would realize they were but pawns in a chess game played at their expense.*"

Nicholas kept his eyes closed as he asked a question out loud, "The horse marauders we met were followers of the Daemons?"

"*Yes,*" Tenzin responded and paused, "*They were soldiers of the Daemons' army and there are more to follow.*"

'Great,' Nicholas thought.

"*The problem is not that the Daemons have followers. It is that they know there is a new Magus in the realm. They know of you, and know who you are, and what you may be capable of,*" she paused. "*This is their greatest worry. They will do everything they can to remove you from the equation.*"

"Well, that certainly takes a load off my mind."

"*Your mind is your greatest asset, Nicholas Thompson. Do not ever underestimate what you are capable of being,*" said Tenzin firmly. "*There are no limitations in the infinite. Remember that. You create your own reality and this may also impact the reality of others. For now, we are done. Stay on the path and you will fare well.*"

*   *   *

The next morning, Nicholas opened his eyes when he heard Cobie on the satellite cell phone. Her voice was muffled and inaudible. He got up and knocked on Cobie's door. She opened it and motioned for him to come in as she talked on her cell, making arrangements for Rada's IDs. As Cobie terminated the call, Nicholas drew his hand down her cheek to her neck, pushed her long hair away, and kissed her gently in the nape of her neck just below her ear.

"I've been dreaming about doing that all night."

Just as Cobie started to draw nearer to Nicholas for their first kiss, Rada popped in.

"Oh – sorry!"

Embarrassed, Nicholas and Cobie broke their embrace.

"We need to get your photo for an ID... we need to get moving if we're going to make the red-eye tonight." Cobie redirected everyone's attention to the problems at hand.

As Rada and Nicholas left Cobie's room, Cobie murmured, "I know your secret."

*   *   *

Several minutes later, Rada, Nicholas and Cobie met in the living room area.

"It's nice now that we have showered and cleaned up a bit," Nicholas was searching for conversation that would cover the awkwardness he felt.

"Yes, great for you two. Incredible for me. I have never had rain in my room," said Rada. "And there's a gun that shoots hot air. Very interesting."

"Rada, I believe you are going to be exposed to much on this adventure, as I was exposed to much in your home," said Nicholas.

Nicholas considered how amazing it must be for Rada to experience the twenty-first century based on his background and his living with the ancient society. But Nicholas also thought about how much more advanced the members of the Cloister were, at least in the metaphysical sense. Which society was more advanced, really?

Chapter 24

Where the speech is corrupted, the mind is also.

Lucius Annaeus Seneca

Just as Jen was becoming seriously concerned about her brother, she finally heard from him. Nicholas was on his way back to the States. His voice and enthusiasm for life sounded the same, but there was something underlying the sound of his voice she had never heard before; some sort of omniscient undertone, or perhaps just ominous. She wasn't sure what it was, but it seemed that she could feel his presence through the phone lines as if he were staring into her from across the thousands of miles of separation.

He told her he was coming back with a few friends he had made while traveling in the mountains. One was a geophysicist and the other an exchange student.

"I figure if I'm going to be off for the year in the United States, I might as well continue with some research on my own. By bringing Cobie and Rada, I have a colleague and a lab assistant to help with the efforts. Although Cobie is still talking about making some trips up to Yosemite, and the Sierras, I think she might be able to help with some of my own research as well."

'Cobie and Rada,' she thought, 'Sounded like Cobian rada, an evil lizard-monster from Planet X.' They sounded like the words she had written down when she had been hypnotized. She had started to relay to Nicholas the events of her internship, but had been abruptly interrupted by Nicholas' enthusiasm. He wanted to talk and Jen was apparently to listen.

Nicholas did not want to worry Jen with the story of the attack by the assailants, and his death-experience, or his growing feelings for Cobie, so he continued hiding his deep emotions with enthusiasm for performing again. Nicholas was excited about trying some new magical effects at the Magic Castle. "I do miss my good old sleight-of-hand. I think this new magic has dulled my physical dexterity. I need to keep my old magic skills up to par with the new magic I have been practicing. I need to meld them together, form a unique relationship, and nurture them so they're not lost."

Nicholas was on his way back and was already planning to schedule a week at the Magic Castle for later in the month. Nicholas never was one for slowing down to 'smell the roses.'

Jen understood, it was his way. She was just so thankful that he was okay and coming home. She truly did not want to concern Nicholas with her dreams and issues until he was safely back in Los Angeles. She could tell from his voice, that below the enthusiasm there was an undertone of concern too. She would wait to tell her side of the summer.

She also thought his booking at the Magic Castle would be a perfect opportunity for Nicholas to wear the new present she had bought for him. Jen opened the shirt box with the Samurai kimono to repack it for shipping. As she took the kimono out of the box, a small card with tiny precise handwriting read: yakata – Satsuma clan, Boshin War 1868. Could it be possible that this kimono had belonged to an actual samurai warrior from the Boshin War over one hundred years ago? It was this war that opened Japan to the Western world and ended the reign of the Shogunates and the Samurai. Jen believed in karma and synchronicities and thought there was some relationship between her finding this particular robe and the role Nicholas would continue to play in life. He was indeed a warrior in many fashions, but also perhaps the one to open up the world to other ideas, wonders and magic. No wonder it had lured her to purchase it. She carefully packed it in tissue, taped the box, and addressed it to Nicholas. She hoped he would love it as much as she did and wear it the next time he performed.

As Jen put the finishing touches on the package to her brother, Sansa knocked on the guest bedroom door.

"Come on in," Jen offered. Sansa came in and sat on the bed next to her.

"I was speaking with some of my friends at Danny's magic shop this afternoon about the phrase you wrote down. Fortunately, I had a copy and when I showed it to this one magician, he seemed to know what it was. He said it sounded like some Black Magick chants he had heard in the past. Danny thought it might be too, so I kept on asking what it meant and if he knew how to translate it. Both of them said they didn't but they tried to look it up on the Internet. You know how magicians are with a challenge."

Jen was very interested. She put down the package and listened intently. "So, did you find out or not?" she asked anxiously.

Sansa pulled Jen up off the bed and took her into the office. "C'mon, look!"

They entered Sansa's office and while Sansa sat down at the desk, Jen looked over his shoulder at the computer screen. He had located an Enochian language website.

"It's a religious language... Dr. John Dee had something to do with it. It says here that supposedly Angels transmitted the language to him in the 1600's, but the consensus is that the origin of the language is much older than that." He read, "Some Enochian has been found as far back as the invention of the Arabic alphabet, and the origin of the language itself is believed to be one of the oldest in the history of mankind, pre-text or stone tablets. John Dee was just the conduit for the Enochian Keys from the Dark Angels, keys which now serve as the commandments within the 'Satanic Bible'."

Sansa clicked into a different website that read only two words: Enochian Keys. The website had red letters on a black background and contained a list of what was known as the nineteen Enochian keys. Sansa clicked on the different keys and read the Enochian followed by the English translations. None of them matched Jen's phrase, until they opened the 10th Key.

"That's it! What's the English translation?" Jen yelled.

Jen read, **"The thunders of judgment and wrath are numbered. And are harbored in the North."**

Jen turned to Sansa, "So what the hell does that mean – thunders of judgment?"

Sansa was perplexed. "I don't know. And we still don't know whom or where this truly came from. I'm worried. I think we should do some preventative insurance today, Jen."

She looked at Sansa and he continued, "No matter whom it comes from, it shouldn't be giving you nightmares or visions of horrific images. I would like to hypnotize you again and keep these images from having any impact on you. Are you willing?"

Jen thought about it. "Yes, you are right. Whom ever they are from, I don't want them to know what I am seeing. I need the images to go away until we can better understand their meaning."

They adjourned back to the garage studio where Sansa calmed Jen down, hypnotized her and instructed her not to allow these words, images, or thoughts to affect her again.

She woke from the trance feeling very relaxed and although she could recall the words and the images, they were no longer invading her frontal lobe, constantly directing her mind to a place where no one would want to venture. No one, she thought, except maybe her boss, Burton Carrier.

Chapter 25

> His magic is performed with complete
> naturalness, its artistry that of the art that
> conceals art. The consummate skill and
> technique is there but it is never displayed; it is,
> on the contrary, so carefully hidden that the
> performer is applauded not for his nimble-
> fingered dexterity but because he has, with the
> effortless ease of a real magician, exhibited a
> feat of what must be real magic.
>
> Jean Hugard and Frederick Braue, "Expert
> Card Technique," Third Edition in reference to
> Dai Vernon

Cobie had been very successful in procuring legitimate identification for Rada's travel; passport, visa, and even a letter of recommendation from the Geology Professor of the Australian National University, outlining the field studies Rada would complete during his visit to the United States. With all the documents in order, Rada had no trouble boarding the DC-10 with Cobie and Nicholas.

Rada had never experienced flying, except of the astral flavor, until this flight. He bounced back and forth from staring out the window amazed at the amount of water beneath him, watching the movie, and listening to every music channel on his headset. He was like a ten-year old boy on his first trip to Disneyland! He eagerly ate the free peanuts and gulped down the fizzy soda. Nicholas and Cobie, on the other hand, could hardly keep their eyes open and both soon fell asleep after take-off. Cobie's head fell and rested on Nicholas' shoulder.

After more than twenty-four hours and an uneventful layover in Shanghai, the three exhausted travelers de-planed at LAX and took a taxi to Nicholas' house. Rada and Cobie instantly felt at home in the magician's abode.

Later that evening over a bottle of California Cabernet, Nicholas explained the connection between his property and its previous owner, Harry Houdini, the world-renown escape artist. They listened intently to Nicholas as he told them about Houdini's past, how he was influenced by the French magician Jean Eugene Robert-Houdin. Ehric Weisz (Houdini's real name) began calling himself Harry Houdini; paying homage to Robert-Houdin by adding an "i" to his last name and taking the first name of yet another great magician, Harry Kellar.

Harry had apparently died of a ruptured appendix on Halloween in 1926 following a visit backstage by a university student who challenged Houdini's claim of being able to withstand any blow to the stomach. Seeking no medical attention, and continuing his bravado until the pain could not be withstood, Harry succumbed to his death on Halloween night. Houdini had left his wife a secret code that he would use to contact her from the great beyond if there was a possibility to do so.

So, Wilhemina Beatrice Houdini, performed a special séance on the anniversary of his death for the following ten years in an attempt to contact Harry in the great beyond. As far as the world knows, she was never successful in communicating with her deceased husband. Every subsequent Halloween, special séances were held at a variety of locations to continue to try and contact Harry post-mortem. Harry did not appear at any of these events, even to the séances held on Nicholas' property on 'All Hallows Eve'.

"Maybe she wasn't looking in the right place for Harry," said Rada calmly.

*   *   *

In the days that followed their arrival in LA, Nicholas, Rada and Cobie spent most of their evenings in the library. Rada and Cobie loved the library; it was the heart of the house. Or maybe the brains…

The days were very busy with the sights and sounds of Los Angeles as Nicholas tried to share the scenes of the city with his visitors: art galleries, the La Brea Tar Pits, Getty Museum, the Pacific Ocean and Santa Monica Mountains. They all especially loved the mountains, and their hikes on the trails above the city. Nicholas even gave them a personal V.I.P. tour of the Mount Wilson Observatory high above the city. He still had many friends at the observatory doing solar astronomy experiments, so he had special access to the facility. It was at this observatory that Alan Sandage had derived the Hubble constant after years of observations in the Doppler redshift of distant galaxies. It was here where the age of the ever-expanding universe was originally defined by the human race.

On one of their daily outings, they went to the Santa Monica Third Street Promenade. Nicholas purchased some casual wear for Rada, including shorts. Rada had been mostly wearing hand-me-downs from Nicholas up until that point. Rada was in awe of anything and everything, sponging in all he saw, felt and heard. Cobie was a delightful companion and always kept the conversations light and cheery. They were a group of individuals, which had evolved into a triumvirate, feeding off one another's friendship and hope.

Nicholas eventually began to relax but he found that he and Cobie were never alone together. Rada was omnipresent. Was that by Rada's design? Was Rada being over-protective because of Nicholas' near-death experience? They would steal a glance, a touch, a nearness every once in a while. Still, Nicholas recognized that they had strength as a threesome and until the unsettling future was more stable, he needed to be content to leave things as they were. The electricity and vibration was still there between Cobie and himself, just a little more subtle. If their relationship was meant to be, it could only get stronger as they developed their friendship. And he was still not sure he truly wanted a relationship.

Nicholas had saved the best sightseeing for the last. He had booked himself into the Parlour of Prestidigitation at the Magic Castle and was looking forward to showing off a bit for Rada and Cobie. He was dying to combine what he had learned at the Cloister with his mastery of sleight-of-hand techniques.

The Parlour of Prestidigitation was a medium-sized venue combining the intimacy of the close-up gallery with the large-scale stage shows in the Palace. Nicholas decided to begin his act with one of his favorite magical effects that many magicians believed covered the gamut of conjuring knowledge and misdirection; an effect upon which all other magic could be based. This effect was known as the Classic Cups and Balls.

So on the second Monday in September, at 10:00 p.m. after a brief, but elegant introduction of the Magus, the curtains parted in the Parlour of Prestidigitation revealing Nicholas, clad in black from head to foot. He strode forward confidently and sat down at a small green felt covered table. On the table there were three gold cups, stacked one on top of another. Between Nicholas and the cups was a mahogany magic wand with gold tips.

His voice was direct and professorial, "The cups and balls have been the epitome of magical performances for nearly five thousand years. Pictographs of magicians performing the cups and balls from 2600 B.C. have been found on the stone walls in the tombs of Beni Hasan in Egypt. As recently as 1988 Anno Domini, a magician became the World Champion of magic for his performance of the cups and balls while competing against magicians from forty-seven countries. So I ask, why are the cups and balls such a definitive effect in the annals of magic? One reason: Simplicity. The trick is performed with three empty cups."

As he spoke, he picked up the stack of cups, and very slowly showed the audience each was empty as he placed them individually on the table in a row with the opening of the cup face down.

"Another reason is that they portray the basis of all magic; Magic that actually changes the perception of reality as defined by physics."

He picked up the wand with his right hand and began to rub it with the fingers of his other hand as he continued; "The probability of the existence of matter is determined when the act of observation collapses the ethereal wave function into solid form." A small white crocheted ball appeared in his fingertips at the end of the wand. He placed the wand under his left arm as he passed the ball to his right hand and placed it on the top of the cup to his left.

He grabbed the wand again with his right hand and began speaking, "Reality as we know it is actually only a probability; a wave pattern, like a spinning wand, until the mind of the observer freezes the wand causing the reality of the object to materialize at a single point." He spun the wand and tapped his left hand to reveal a second white crocheted ball.

He took the second ball and passed it through the solid base of the middle cup to the tabletop below. "But remember, all that appears solid in this allusive reality, is not."

He picked up the ball from underneath the middle cup and placed it on top of the cup to his right. "And all that appears to be where you believe it to be, is not, because, reality is determined by the act of observation. Before being observed, the where and when of the manifestation of reality is all based on your perception, and imagination." As he spoke these final words, he pointed to the top of the three cups with the wand. There were now three balls, one on top of each cup. The audience was deceived, entertained, and overall pleasantly surprised. They applauded accordingly.

"Contemplate this, the true magical spirit of reality, as I perform my version of the Cups and Balls."

As he finished his proclamation, the organ strains of Pink Floyd's "Shine On You Crazy Diamond" began. Oooohs and aahhs of the audience, accompanied by occasional laughter, transformed the magical routine into a bewildering and awesome illusion. *Wonder* prevailed.

For his finale, the music came to a crescendo and Nicholas lifted the cups to reveal three large crystal balls beneath. The applause began, but he raised his hands and began to speak.

"The cups and balls may truly be one of the oldest effects in the history of magic, but I would like to demonstrate some of the 21st century advancements in sleight-of-hand which collectively fuse together the art of magic, quantum physics and eastern philosophy."

As he spoke, he put the cups and crystal balls on another small table off to the side of the stage.

"The Japanese Koan says, 'A tree falling in the woods heard by no one makes no sound,' which is analogous to the Heisenberg Uncertainty Principle in quantum mechanics which alludes to the ambiguity of substance. This can be demonstrated magically, with one coin," and a coin appeared at his finger tips, "or four," and three others appeared in his other hand, "which when not being observed, do not truly exist in the phase-space that you might expect." He paused and then continued, "So for your consideration, here is an example of what I call Quantum Prestidigitation."

He placed the four Liberty half-dollars into the four corners of an imaginary square on the felt table top and covered two of the coins with his hands as the music began: a fast violin solo. He moved his hands slowly above the coins and they appeared and vanished and regrouped for the next two minutes beneath his hands. It was a beautifully choreographed routine, based on John Born's *Matrix God's Way*, which he executed flawlessly.

The audience was stunned, allowing him a chance to step back behind the curtain and reappear wearing the handsome black and burgundy Samurai yakata and holding an Oriental silk foulard. The yakata was the gift from Jen.

With a flourish, Nicholas displayed the brightly colored, intricately designed foulard. A silver ball five inches in diameter, floated from beneath the scarf. Timed to a selection of music from 'Cirque Du Soleil' called Fanfares, the Zombie Ball became animated, taking on an aggressive yet elusive personality of its own. Could an inanimate object assume anthropomorphic qualities? At first Nicholas' Zombie effect resembled that of any other polished magician; but as the music intensified the trick deviated from the norm.

The silver ball rested on the foulard, which was pulled taut by the Magus. Slowly the ball began to rise above the foulard and revolve very slowly around Nicholas' head and body. Nicholas stood perfectly still staring toward the back of the theater. The magicians in the audience were no longer just being entertained; they were actually stunned!

Suddenly the music accelerated and The Magus began to perform a kata-like routine with the ball as his shadowboxing partner. He punched at the ball and it jumped back. He put down the foulard and picked up a Samurai sword. The ball floated in front of him. It shifted up and down slightly as if supported by blowing air. Nicholas swung the sword at the ball and it feigned up and out of the way. He swung back and again it evaded the strike. It was a beautiful dance of attack and avoidance between the Magus and the ball.

With one final spinning slice the act concluded and the music faded away. To the roar of the audience, the Magus bowed to his worthy opponent. The ball, in turn dropped slightly in an arch towards the Magus in imitation of a bow as well. Nicholas turned towards the audience and bowed to them, in unison with the ball that dipped to the spectators.

He slowly turned towards the ball and reached out with his arm. The ball came to rest gently on his hand. He picked up the foulard and covered the ball. Its shape was still apparent under the foulard but when Nicholas pulled the scarf away the magical ball had vanished! In its place was a solitary white rose. He again bowed towards the audience, this time solo, and a tremendous applause prevailed. He handed the rose to Cobie in the first row.

Nicholas was invigorated and pleased with the response he had received for the evening's performance. He had decided to incorporate more of his 'new' magic into his routine, magic from the Cloister, blending the old and the new, the sleight-of-hand and the mental, and felt he had been very successful in this capacity. He knew magic was more about wonder than about technique. Regardless of how the effects were performed, it was the mystery and the ensuing wonder of the audience that was the ultimate objective. Belief in the impossible was just a perk.

Nicholas joined Cobie and Rada at the Palace Bar. The hustle of the Castle patrons while they attempted to maneuver between showrooms was overwhelming for Rada, who had backed into the last chair at the bar. He was looking a little out of place and even a bit frightened by the commotion.

"You are dangerously talented!" Cobie flirted. She had placed the white rose in her hair.

"Why thank you!" Nicholas bowed to her, delighted. Rada had nodded in agreement.

Cobie leaned over to whisper in Nicholas' ear, "I think I should take him home and come back to pick you up after your last show. This crowd's obviously getting to him. I don't think he's used to so many people."

Nicholas could see that Rada was flinching as people came and went in front of him. Many of the magician members were yelling to Nicholas as they walked by, "Great show, Magus!" And Rada seemed to cower a bit back into his chair. It was definitely too much for the neophyte among the L.A. populous.

Nicholas spoke to Rada, "My friend, I think maybe you have had enough excitement and magic for one night. You think you might be ready to head home?"

Rada nodded, "Yes, actually, I think that might be a good idea."

Nicholas turned to Cobie, "Okay – you think you know how to get home and come back? I could take a taxi home."

"I'm a great navigator and observer. I'll find it." She pulled Rada from the corner, "See you in a couple of hours, Magus," she winked, and led Rada toward the exit door of the Castle.

Nicholas spent a little while in the library after his last performance of the evening to pass the time before Cobie picked him up. He wanted to research some old lecture notes from his sage in the magic community, Eugene Burger for an effect he was interested in performing. Several magicians approached him as he flipped through the notes. They stopped and shook hands, "I've never see anything like your performance tonight."

One said, "So where the hell have you been studying all summer? Was that like from Jeff McBride's Master Master Master class?"

"Seriously, who have you been studying with?"

Nicholas was cautious, "I've had the privilege of studying with many mentors and all I can say is, I'm proud to be able to combine many different arts into one performance."

By the time his admirers had left and Nicholas had collected his props and kimono, the Magic Castle was all but deserted. The bartenders were finishing their final duties of closing up the liquor cabinets, counting their tips and taking their cash drawers to the main office. All the other magicians had left. He carried the black bag with his props in one hand, and the clear plastic garment bag containing the kimono in the other. He exited the Castle through a side door by the magicians' library and headed towards the parking lot where he had promised to meet Cobie.

As Nicholas passed through the side alley of the original 1908 house, a figure stepped out of the shadows. Nicholas turned to his left and saw two more darkly dressed men appear from behind a large recycle bin. The two of them had knives and the one in the center pointed a gun at Nicholas.

"I have no money." Nicholas declared. He dropped his black bag to the ground behind him and hooked the garment bag on the lattice wall to his left. He stood in a casual yet, "get-ready" stance.

"We know who you are, Mr. Magi. We cannot afford to have you threaten our plans," said a strong voice to his left.

"I'm sorry, what did you say?" Nicholas asked with confidence.

"We are here to finish what was started a while ago," responded the apparent leader.

Nicholas moved slowly and responded calmly, "Ah, but the real question is: Has it truly begun?" The Zombie ball began to rise out of the black bag behind his back. The ball rose up his spine and floated behind his shoulder blades.

"Trust us Dr. Thompson, it will end tonight. We have been directed to succeed where the other team has failed."

"I see, so you are associated with the Others." He looked toward the ground and shook his head. "Those poor men."

The leader's eyes changed. They seemed to be turning black, as if the pupils had grown over the irises. A deep guttural voice rose from within.

"I know what you did to our friends, Nicholas Thompson. Your future ends now."

Nicholas responded, "Well… then… you are misinformed!"

The leader shook his head as if to reconnect the brain cells with the body.

"Why don't you just have a ball," Nicholas responded.

The Zombie ball shot over Nicholas' shoulder hitting the gun, knocking it out of the shooter's hand as it fired into the air. The ball then shot up and hit the thug clean in his face, sending him sprawling. When the ball hit the gun, Nicholas simultaneously

179

attacked and threw a spinning wheel kick into the face of the second assailant. His foot hit the mugger just as the ball hit the first man in the face. Both muggers dropped to the ground and neither of them would be getting up anytime soon.

The third assailant looked at his friends and ran. The Zombie ball rose above the face of the man it took down, and followed after the running thug. It encircled him several times then suddenly stopped right in front of his face. The third mugger froze and stared at it. The ball remained motionless. The thug smiled at the ball as if to say, this is cute. Suddenly the ball hit the mugger in the forehead and he slumped to the ground.

"As I said, better yet, have a ball," Nicholas said calmly looking at the carnage. Cobie rounded the corner looking for Nicholas.

"What's all this?" she asked as she stepped over one of the assailants to get to Nicholas.

Nicholas resigned himself to the fact that he had been found, "It appears the Others know I'm here."

Chapter 26

*Responsibility is measured, not by the amount
of injury resulting from wrong action, but by the
distinctness with which conscience has the
opportunity of distinguishing between the right
and the wrong.*

Frederick William Robertson

Jen's nightmares had diminished to being almost non-existent, happily coinciding with Nicholas' return to Los Angeles. Jen felt that maybe she had had separation anxiety from Nicholas and had created the horrific images herself.

After playing phone tag day after day, Jen finally reached Nicholas and relayed her nightmare experience in the lab. The diminished urgency of the images Jen had seen made her feel foolish.

Burton had given them even more than two days off. Jen had not had any repeat sessions of the Quantum Telepathy experiment for the last week. Burton seemed to be avoiding the lab, his co-workers and Jen. That was okay with her. For once working on the specifications for the experiment was a preferred task. Her internship was nearly over and she was extremely happy to ponder her return home and meeting Nicholas' new friends.

Jen was quite surprised to learn that the week before she was to head back to LA, Burton wanted to continue with the Quantum Telepathy experiment. He seemed especially gruff and rude on the first morning, practically shoving Jen into the isolation room for her meditation and telepathy exercise.

For Burton, this was the week of action. Anan'kra had transferred the required software needed to take control of the military assets, as well as the commercial airlines. It was sapient software capable of analyzing and making knowledge-based decisions within the current systems software. Burton needed to cause a comprehensive shut down of Washington communications and the U.S. government. He would take complete control of the forces in the sky and many of the ground resources as well. All government resource control would be routed through Mount Weather, putting him in charge of all of the necessary military assets to prepare for 'The Coming' of Anan'kra and the Others. Their initial headquarter preference was to be subterranean and Mt. Weather was the perfect facility for this effort.

He was concerned though that there may have been a leak of information in the telepathy experiment with Jen, and he needed to make sure there were no loose ends. No one could know the plan. He needed to be sure, so he would try one more time with the experiment and if she were receiving and interpreting any of his plans, he was prepared to eradicate the loose ends.

Jen sat as calmly as she could in the solitary confinement of the experiment room. She was actually scared. She did not want this to start all over again. However, the visions came fast and furious again but this time, there were more of them. Jen saw a strange-looking beast. She couldn't identify it, but it seemed like the blending of many animals in one. And it was not pretty. The same Enochian words in her cerebral cortex underlay the entire plan of Burton, Anan'kra and the revolution. The phrase was clear now; part of the tenth Enochian key and Jen knew it translated to 'The thunder of wrath doth slumber in the North.' Although she did not really know what that meant, Jen saw what Burton was planning and she was scared.

She sat quietly in her chair this time though. She used her martial arts training to remain focused and still, not surprised. She must not let them know she knew. She had to be strong; she had to act as if nothing were wrong, that nothing had been communicated to her. She had to block all thoughts both coming and going so that absolutely no one could read her mind.

Burton opened the door to Jen's room, "Did you receive anything?"

Jen appeared chipper, "No – nothing... sorry."

As soon as she was released, she bounded out of the chair and went to her office to begin reading the specification manual again. When she knew she was not watched, she picked up the phone and dialed for a long distance connection. She realized it was imperative she reach Nicholas. He would know what to do. He would know what all of this meant and he would be able to get her out of this predicament and rescue her, rescue the world. She truly felt this might be the case. Even the lengthy conversations she had on the phone with Nicholas as of late had revealed he was part of something bigger now. She truly believed he might be able to help. Somehow, he gave her an inkling of hope. She just wanted to finish her internship and leave Mt. Weather, never to return again.

But first she needed to talk to her brother, The Magus.

Chapter 27

Nurture your mind with great thoughts; to believe in the heroic makes heroes.

Benjamin Disraeli

Nicholas meditated in silence on the floor of his library, eyes closed and breath controlled. He had been meditating since his college days, but since going to the Cloister, his focus and attention had become more attuned to the universe around him and his connections to it. He could feel the presence of his companions, Cobie and Rada, in the house. He could sense the movement of air through the open window on the second story. He could feel the spider weaving her web above the Vampire anthologies in the horror section of the alcove. He felt attuned to all within his home and beyond. He felt connected to all.

As he focused his meditation beyond the peace of his immediate surroundings, letting himself travel deeper into the ether, he began to sense an evil presence. He couldn't pin it down exactly, but he sensed a dark force pervading the goodness he felt in his house. The peace he felt when he began the meditation now became overwhelmed by a sinister darkness.

The phone rang.

Nicholas opened his eyes in a flash. Escaping the dark feeling, he responded to the reality of the external sound.

"Nicholas Thompson," he said as he picked up the receiver.

"Nick, it's Jen." She was whispering, afraid of being heard.

"Hi sis, how's it going in the covert world of national security?"

"Well, not so good."

Nicholas sensed the darkness again in the ether.

"What's up?"

"I don't know how to tell you this or how you can help, but the guy I'm working for ... well ... I think he may be planning something really bad. And I mean *really bad*."

"What do you mean?"

Her answer was rapid-fire, "His name is Dr. Burton Carrier and he's been working on some really cool stuff I can't talk about, but, I overheard him... well, I didn't really overhear him... I know he is communicating with someone outside our group."

"What are you talking about, Jen?"

"He was talking about controlling missiles and jets and all sorts of stuff in a coup against the U.S. government."

Nicholas' first instinct was to say, "Yeah right." But he sensed something deeper. He felt a twinge of fear, and what he could only describe as intense disharmony within his senses. He believed she was not only telling the truth, but this was somehow related to his own destiny as described by Tenzin.

"I believe you, Jen. I think I need to come to D.C. and see if there is anything I can do."

Jen did not believe it was going to be that easy, "Nick, seriously, I am not kidding."

"I know Jen. I truly do believe you," he said confidently with feeling.

"Nick, I don't know what to do, or what you could do, but even if you can get me out of here ... well, that would at least be a relief."

"We're on our way."

"*We're?*"

"Yes, I think it would be prudent on my part to bring Rada and Cobie, the friends I made while abroad. They have been tremendous help to me and from what you just told me, we will need all the help we can get."

"We're on our way," and he hung up the phone.

Rada entered the library and saw the look on Nicholas' face.

"Something's wrong."

"Yes – my sister's in trouble. There is something big going on in her covert world and we have to get her back home. This may involve us once again with the Others ... I sensed a sinister force at work somewhere out there while I was meditating just now. Will you come to Washington D.C. with me? I'm going to ask Cobie to join us as well. I have a feeling we all have a part to play in stemming the tide of this dark conflict."

*   *   *

Cobie, Rada and Nicholas sat on the plane to D.C. from Los Angeles. The plane was full, and Rada, of course, got the window seat. He had been staring out the window the past four hours because this was different from the flight from India; this was a flight over the North American continent. He was fascinated with the terrain below and the vastness of uninhabited land in the United States.

"I assumed it was like one big city. It always felt like so many souls in one place," he said to no one in particular.

Cobie and Nicholas spoke quietly of what they might do to stop what was being planned. But they did not have enough information. Their initial goal would be to get Jen away from the situation. Nicholas realized it could be a real problem if someone inside the government had any semblance of the powers he himself had, especially if that someone had a propensity for evil. He wasn't positive but he thought that Jen's boss, Burton Carrier, might be one of 'the Others' with a very strong penchant for evil. He might even be one of the leaders of the group. But, it was too early to tell.

"I think the first thing to do is to get my sister out of Mt. Weather and away from Burton Carrier. Then we'll contact the authorities, like the FBI or CIA or whomever," said Nicholas outlining his choice of action.

"I agree. You said Jen is meeting us at the airport? From then on she should never leave our side," responded Cobie.

Two swarthy-looking men seated in front of Nicholas and Cobie seemed to be taking an interest in their conversation. Nicholas thought one man reacted when Nicholas mentioned Burton Carrier's name, or maybe it was at the mention of the CIA. He whispered to Cobie to change their topic of conversation.

Nicholas watched as one of the men passed the second one a silver cigar tube. The second man stood up and retrieved his overnight satchel from the overhead compartment. After rummaging through the larger section of the bag, he withdrew a small case containing a metal hair dryer and a small cosmetic bag with a zippered top. Placing the bag on his seat, he returned the satchel to the overhead compartment.

He then took the hair dryer to the back restroom. Inside, the man unscrewed the lids of the metal cigar case on both ends, and unhooked the hair dryer nozzle, which left only the handle and trigger of the dryer. The man smiled to himself at just how easy it was to sneak what seemed like and ordinary hair dryer onto the plane. He screwed the cigar tube into the hair dryer trigger completing the assembly of a very lethal weapon. The metal nozzle of the hair dryer was stuffed with bullets and he retrieved them, loading them into the gun.

The man flushed the toilet, washed his hands and placed the gun in his jacket pocket. He threw the hair dryer nozzle into the trashcan to the left of the sink and covered it with the towel he had used to dry his hands.

The first man had opened the cosmetic bag and begun fidgeting with the objects inside. As the second man from the bathroom got to the row in front of Nicholas, the first man stood up and joined the second one. He had fashioned a small but ominous-looking bomb out of plastic explosives, a battery and wire that would explode on contact if thrown.

Nicholas' cat-like instincts took over when just as the second man pulled the gun out of his jacket pocket and began to take aim at Nicholas, he jumped up and lunged at the men. They were so startled; they stumbled backwards, turned and ran down the aisle toward the first class compartment.

The curtains to the first class were closed so high paying customers could sleep, work on their laptops and drink free cocktails without being bothered by the common folk. As the two men got to the first class curtains, the first one turned quickly and revealed his hand-made bomb to the passengers in economy class. The second man pulled back the curtain separating the first class passengers, surprising a flight attendant who was serving cocktails in the aisle.

"Remain seated," screamed the first man with the bomb visibly in his hand. "If you don't do as we say, you will die. Don't think we are incapable of killing you all. The explosives in this bomb have the capability of blowing quite a large hole in the airplane. Most of you know if that happens, the suction will take all of you into the atmosphere, and the plane will most certainly crash."

As he spoke, the gunman in first class rushed toward the flight attendant. He grabbed the metal coffee pot from the service tray and hit her hard in the face. She careened over into row one and a first class passenger caught her. The gunman shoved the service cart into the attendant's area sending ice and drinks flying through the first class cabin.

As the gunman reached the pilot's door, he shot two bullets at the lock on the door to the pilot's compartment. The door sprung open when he kicked it in. The co-pilot reached under his seat, retrieved a concealed handgun and turned toward the gunman. The gunman was prepared, and shot the co-pilot before he could take aim.

Next, he pointed his gun at the chest of the pilot; he fired twice. The bullets passed through the pilot into the rear of his chair. Puffs of smoke emitted from the two bullet holes in the chair. He fell over dead onto the floor of the cabin along with the co-pilot.

Hearing the gunshots, passengers panicked. Most were too frightened to move and simply cowered in their seats mumbling prayers and holding hands. The gunman picked up the co-pilot's gun and threw it down the aisle to the other assailant.

"We need to take some initiative and resolve the situation," Nicholas declared looking at Cobie and Rada.

"Although I do not think they are the evil we may be pursuing, these men are not good men," said Rada.

As he finished the phrase, Nicholas stood and stepped into the aisle.

"And what part of "remain seated" did you not understand?" the second gunman said to Nicholas. He pointed the pilot's gun at Nicholas' chest and fired without hesitation.

Nicholas could feel the pressure of the bullet pushing the air out of its way as it approached his chest, but time had slowed down. He could sense the speed and the power behind its initial explosion, and by feeling its power and its place in the universe, he could feel his own control over the bullet.

Nicholas pushed with his inner self toward the projectile. The bullet slowed, then slowed some more. He pushed harder and the bullet stopped, floating in front of his body in mid-air.

The gunman could not comprehend the bullet's behavior. Confusion turned to fear as he pulled the trigger again. Nicholas could sense the mechanism within the gun and inhibited the explosion of gunpowder behind the bullet. There was no explosion. The bullet jammed.

The gunman from the pilot's cabin heard the shot and ran through first class with his gun pointed toward economy.

Nicholas pushed and he pushed hard. The gunman in economy flew back in the air as if shot by a bazooka. He folded over in pain and collided with the second gunman who fired his pistol instinctively upon impact. As they both hit the floor, the first class passengers swooped in on them, pinning them down.

Pandemonium ensued. People screamed. There was a rush for the cockpit from those not restraining the gunmen, as the passengers began to realize no one was flying the plane.

Nicholas sat down next to Cobie, trying to think things out.

"Hmmm, that was creative and intriguing," said Cobie coyly to Nicholas in response to his handling of the terrorists, trying to hide her nerves.

"You have done well Dr. Thompson. Your lessons have been well learned," added Rada.

"Yes, but we still have a major situation at hand. As you may have noticed the plane no longer has a pilot, and we do have to land at some point," replied Nicholas.

"Ah yes, not a problem, Dr. Thompson," said Cobie recovering her confidence, "I am an accomplished pilot. I have clocked over four thousand hours of air time."

She paused as Nicholas took in her statement. "I had to find my way to some pretty out-of-the-way places as a geologist and learning to fly seemed to be the best way to accomplish my research. Not to mention I love to fly."

"There's got to be a bit of a difference between flying a small airplane and a commercial aircraft." Nicholas was apprehensive.

"Same principle, different size." Cobie answered assuredly.

"Well, I knew there was a reason I brought you along. I figured it couldn't be for your good looks, brains and sense of humor," said Nicholas with a smile.

He turned towards the aisle as the flight attendant rushed toward the cockpit to jump in the midst of the chaos.

"Miss!" he yelled over the commotion, "She can fly this plane!" he said pointing at Cobie.

The flight attendant stopped in her tracks and everyone around them turned to look at Cobie.

"You can fly??!!" the flight attendant yelled back toward Cobie.

"Yes ma'am," Cobie responded confidently in her Australian accent. "I am a pilot."

"Hurry, follow me," said the flight attendant, grabbing Cobie by the arm and dragging her from her seat.

Nicholas and Rada followed Cobie and the flight attendant toward the cockpit. The pummeled, and most likely deceased, terrorists had been placed in the lavatory, naked. There was not a lot of compassion these days for terrorists.

"Pilot coming through!" yelled the flight attendant as she moved down the aisle with Cobie in tow.

All eyes were on Cobie.

As they approached the cockpit, the first class flight attendant pointed to the pilots behind her and said in a state of shock, "They're both dead."

The finality of the statement and the tears in her eyes defined the situation.

Cobie looked firmly at her and said, "I am a pilot. I cannot bring them back, but I do believe I can fly and land this plane. Let's move them out of here and let me see what I can do with this bird."

The flight attendant and Nicholas moved the bodies of the pilots from the cockpit. Cobie sat down and put the headset on. Rada kept watch from the pilot's door as the flight attendants tried to calm everyone down. Nicholas looked to Rada for support as he took a seat in the co-pilot's chair.

Cobie heard the concerns of air traffic immediately, "American flight one-nineteen, are you there? What is your situation? Please report your status."

Cobie responded, "This is Dr. Cobie Dulan. I'm a passenger on this flight. Both the pilots have been killed. The terrorists have been subdued. I am a pilot and I believe, with your help, I can bring us down."

"This is Reagan National air-traffic control. Your current position is 97 miles west of the District. We were informed of the terrorists by the pilots about 15 minutes ago, and we apologize but cannot be sure you are a pilot with good intentions."

Cobie was afraid of that. How were they to know she was not a terrorist planning on piloting the plane into the Capital or other prime target?

"Can we speak with the flight attendant, Linda Grabowski please?" the voice said over the headset.

Cobie turned and yelled to the flight attendant.

"Are you Linda Grabowski?"

She nodded.

"They want to talk with you."

Cobie handed the headset over to her.

"This is Linda Grabowski."

"Linda this is air-traffic control at Reagan National, do you know the security code word?"

"I do. It's 'passive one.'"

"Confirmed. Are you okay? Is this woman really a pilot?"

"I believe she is. And if not, I hate to say it, but we're screwed. It was her companion that took down the terrorists. The passenger list shows her as an Australian citizen, a geology professor I heard her tell another passenger."

"Okay, put her back on and try to calm down the passengers. We all need to do our jobs now."

Cobie put on the headset and as she turned her head to assess the airplane's control panel, she noticed in her peripheral vision the fighter jets on either side of the plane.

"It appears I'm getting an escort. Thanks for the hospitality," she said.

"Only a precaution. They will guide you to the runway."

"I understand."

"First step Dr. Dulan, is to take the plane off autopilot."

Cobie switched the autopilot to off as she held the steering mechanism, known as the yoke, tightly in her grasp. She was prepared to take over the controls. However, as she tested its responsiveness by trying to pull it slightly back and to the right, the yoke was unresponsive and continued to turn and rise and lower on its own.

"Houston, I think we have a problem."

"Dr. Dulan, we are experiencing multiple difficulties at this time. The F-16 pilots have lost control of their planes. The news reporters have just announced that several missile silos have become active as…" The communication turned to static on the headset.

Nicholas could see there was a problem from the expression on Cobie's face.

"Cobie, what's up?" he said concerned.

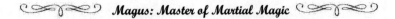

She looked uncomfortable and said, "I think we may not be able to save your sister, or anyone else for that matter. I think the war we were planning to prevent is underway. We are too late.

Chapter 28

Observation killed the cat.

Erwin Schrödinger

Burton was prepared for anything and for everything. He wanted it all and could feel it coming now just barely beyond his reach. He had received the control software he needed to assume complete autonomy over the pentagon's war machines. He was ready, willing and able. His passion for more power was finally going to come true. It was all about him. Yes, Anan'kra and the 'Others' were a big part of the picture, but for now it was all B.C., Burton Carrier. He was in control, and there was nothing that could stop him. Not only would he be powerful, but Anan'kra had also promised him secrets to the universe. The true secrets! Not the petty quantum dominations he had been pursuing. Yeah sure, Quantum Physics was part of the answer, but there was so much more. So much more, and it was all going to be revealed. So yes, it was all about him, Burton Carrier, the Great.

There had been just one small 'burp' in the gastric plan of revolution. Jen Thompson, he realized, had received bits and pieces of the plan through their quantum telepathy experiment. He also realized that it was he, who had told her. Not on purpose of course, but even so, he should have known that the quantum communication was going to work, heck it was already working with Anan'kra! He should have known better than to let her into his mind.

Alas, one small 'burp' for man, while he took one huge 'gulp' against all of mankind.

So, he had decided to call her and told her they had a major breakthrough in the quantum communication experiments and would she please hurry down to the lab.

And she came. Foolish girl.

195

He told her he needed to try one more experiment with just the two of them.

She looked concerned but agreed.

He sat her down in her room of solitary confinement. He said to her as he shut her into the room, "I know you know my plans, Jen. That is why I have invited you here to watch as I take control of the world, beginning with our own government. You are going to watch as I choose which commercial airplanes to crash into government and commercial sites that I have picked for my own pleasure."

She yelled "No!" as she ran towards the door.

He slammed it shut. She screamed and banged on the window. She picked up her chair and threw it at the door. It was secure; unlike the rest of the country.

Nicholas would be on one of those planes, she thought, Nicholas, her dear brother, who was coming to help her, to get her out of this situation. She knew better than to have come to the lab alone with Burton! But she thought, just maybe, she could have delayed Burton from his plot. She was so wrong.

She would have to sit and watch as Burton Carrier performed the most heinous act ever attempted against the U.S. government. She had listened to Nicholas' lectures on quantum physics, and realized just then, that her observation would make it a reality and there was nothing she could do but watch.

Chapter 29

> *Behavior influences consciousness. Right behavior means right consciousness. Our attitude here and now influences the entire environment: our words, actions, ways of holding and moving ourselves, they all influence what happens around us, and inside us.*

Taisen Deshimaru

Nicholas looked at Cobie calmly and said, "My turn to have a try at the wheel."

"You can't fly!" she replied emphatically.

"Well, that's a matter of interpretation," he answered knowingly. "Let me get the feel of the situation. It couldn't hurt." He put on the other headset.

"Ya never know," she said. "It appears we might need a little magic to survive. So be my guest Professor, have a go at it."

Nicholas looked into Cobie's eyes and rested his hand over her hand. Once again he felt that unmistakable surge of electric energy. He turned to the controls, grabbed the yoke, listened to the static and closed his eyes.

He could hear the static and he could feel the lack of power he had over the movement of the yoke in front of him. The steering device was moving to the beat of a different drum, and it was not his. He silenced his mind and focused on the communication network and the steering column. He listened to the static and found beneath the crackle, a low hum that connected to the yoke.

He lowered his head with his eyes shut and focused on the hum. He began to feel the link between the two, the hum and the controls, and he could sense the RF link to the plane. It was a thread of energy flowing into the communication link, which connected the plane to the outside world of electronic devices. It was the connection to the plane from a satellite and to the ground.

He followed this humming thread in his head and let his mind open to the communication links between the airplane and the geostationary satellite. He followed it through the Traveling Wave Tube Amplifiers on the bird, and back down the comm-link to the ground station that was outside of the District of Columbia. Then he bounced from the ground station through the landlines to a terminal underneath the ground at Mt. Weather.

It was here at Mount Weather that Nicholas found the source of the hum. He could sense the entire communication link as a holistic experience and once his mind opened up to this network, he began to feel more. He sensed the whole communication network as a web of influence throughout the universe.

In a brief moment he could feel the communication links through the MilStar satellites to the F-16s and to the missile silos preparing to fire on the White House, the Capital and the Pentagon. He could sense the complete web of radio frequency communication everywhere. He could not limit the scope of his control. He could feel the links to the deep space probes, and even sensed the messages en route from Voyager at the heliopause and the most recent Mars mission roving on the planet's surface.

The expansion of his being was throughout the solar system. He felt connected to it all through the links of radio frequency communications. It was a pleasant omniscient feeling, but more than he felt he could control. He was beginning to overload with information as his experience continued to grow.

He knew it was only a matter of time before he lost control. He needed to push back through the network. He needed to push a pulse back through the link. He wasn't sure what would happen, but he thought just one good push might shut down the source. Just a push.

He focused, and pushed back on the communication link to the plane. With his entire mind, he pushed an electronic pulse, just a

reversal of the incoming energy with a little extra 'oomph', back up through the communication satellite, through the electronic systems and back down from the satellites antenna to the ground station. And from the ground station, he followed the pulse in an ever-increasing snowball of electrons along the underground cables towards the source, gathering force and more energy along the way. Apparently, his 'oomph' was a little more than he had planned. The force now had its own mass and in this capacity its own gravitational pull on the electrons around it in the wires. It grew in power as it flowed deep underground toward the control room at Mount Weather where Dr. Burton Carrier sat at his console focused on the task at hand, and on his future on the planet and in the universe. He knew his reality was about to change, but his anticipated perception of the variation was also about to deviate from his original plan. In a Big Way.

Chapter 30

The way to solve the conflict between human values and technology needs is not to run away from technology. That's impossible. The way to resolve the conflict is to break down the barriers of dualistic thought that prevent a real understanding of what technology is - not an exploitation of nature, but a fusion of nature and the human spirit into a new kind of creation that transcends both.

Robert Pirsig

Burton Carrier saw his entire console of equipment visually alter. It appeared as if everything in his vision pulsed with a powerful wave. The desk was no longer a hardened piece of material, nor the computer nor the keyboard, but a plasma capable of distorting with the pulse of energy that was being pushed from afar.

Solid matter rippled and Burton threw off his headphones as a deep sound blew out the speakers within them. His head rang with the resonating reverberations and his eyes could not fathom the vision in front of him. His computer imploded and then exploded under the pressure, as did the screen and the cables along the ground. The entire room of electronic devices vomited energy into the lab. It was not a pretty site as Dr. Carrier dove across the room to hide under a table.

The electronic bolt on the office door where Jen was locked away exploded as well. It had been connected to the main computer in the room and everything connected to the main computer was in complete spasmodic turmoil. She jumped up as she saw the computer screen explode and ran out of the room where she had been locked away, and through the maelstrom of debris as it flew across the main room. She absorbed a powerful hit to the right side of her head when a connector from a cable blasted forth from the wall. A CD flew before her face like a ninja throwing-star and stuck in the wall to her left. She opened the door exiting the lab and ran into the hallway where the security guards were already gathering.

The door slammed behind her as the room appeared to take a breath inwards. The entire room caved in with the inhalation, and the walls cracked and blistered into the vacuum. Jen's head bled as she looked at the security guards in fear and relief. They were known as the "helping hands." They seemed to live in the walls and at the first sign of any security breach they appeared, like magic. She had seen them once before in their black jump suits carrying M-16s when she had incorrectly entered her code for entrance into the lab three times in a row.

"He's in there!" she yelled.

"Dr. Carrier?" they responded.

"Yes, this is his fault. He's the one causing all this."

As she finished her sentence, her eyes rolled back in her head and she collapsed onto the ground unconscious.

The explosions ended as quickly as they had begun. The guards entered the lab. It was a disaster; the walls and ceiling were cracked and blistered, and every electronic device in the room was burnt and smoldered. The electronic connections to the walls had completely melted and were now fused to the imploded structure. The lab was completely devastated.

*   *   *

They searched for Dr. Carrier but he had disappeared. The external cipher lock had revealed that the last person to code in had, in fact, been Dr. Carrier, but he was no longer in the room. And he had not coded out. There was only one entrance and exit. Burton Carrier had disappeared.

*   *   *

The FBI and the CIA would follow up with a very large-scale investigation but to no avail. Burton Carrier had indeed vanished. The entire incident had been tied to him and his lab, but how he took control and why, they could not establish. All of the historical data and in-situ electronics had been destroyed in the lab. There was no real evidence besides Jen Thompson's story to convict him. Regardless, they could not find Burton anywhere. Any evidence of his continued existence had dissipated.

*   *   *

Jen Thompson woke up in the hospital with her brother at her side.

"Well, it's about time you decided to re-join the human race," he said with a little smirk.

"Hi bro," she said with some difficulty as she tried to focus her eyes. She felt nauseous and had a heck of a headache.

"So, how'd we do?" she asked through the fog.

"Well, we thwarted your boss' plans, thanks to you."

"Thanks to me? Well, that's sweet, but all I know is the lab exploded and …"

"Oh that," said Nicholas with a slight hint of ownership. "Oh I helped with that, but without your phone call this would have all ended differently. And not in a good way."

"I don't understand," she said, but realized her head hurt a bit too much right now to care.

"That's okay sis, take it easy. I know your head is pounding. I can see it in your eyes. Just relax for now."

She closed her eyes as the throbbing enveloped her head in pain.

"I made reservations at the Thompson Tahoe retreat, and we will all be taking a much needed break."

She grimaced in pain, but questioned, "We all?"

"My buddies that I met in Pakistan. Call them my cohorts in magic. Without them, Burton Carrier would have been a well-known entity at this point. They helped immensely. In some ways they do not even know yet."

Nicholas reached out and put his hand on his sister's head.

"Just relax, sis," he said as he rested his palm on her forehead and closed his eyes. "All is as it should be, and all will be explained, and all will be where it needs to be in the future."

He opened his eyes, and removed his hand from her head. Her head pain was gone. She felt relaxed and calm. She thought she heard a low-decibel hum vibrating in the ether of her room.

Chapter 31

> *The known is finite, the unknown infinite;*
> *intellectually we stand on an islet in the midst of*
> *an illimitable ocean of inexplicability. Our*
> *business in every generation is to reclaim a*
> *little more land.*

T.H. Huxley

Nicholas and Jen had not used the cabin at Lake Tahoe since their parents had died. They had retained ownership but it served solely as a rental property for the income. Staying at the cabin would have been too painful a reminder of summers long past. From their births through college, their parents would retreat to the cabin on the lake for what they called "their creative periods" for the whole summer vacation. It was a great escape from their apparently un-creative life in Los Angeles.

The cabin was on the lake, nestled in the pines along the bank. It had a dock extending out into the water about forty feet. It was the perfect escape from the tumultuous environment they had been thrust into, and they all decided to take complete advantage of its availability.

Nicholas was tired, but he was also relaxed. He sat alone on the edge of the dock looking out across the lake as the sun set in the western horizon. As the sun lowered behind the Sierras, the orange-red line of solar reflection slowly diminished across the lake. Nicholas slumped in exhaustion looking at the water, thinking. He reached into his jacket pocket and removed a deck of cards. He took the cover off and began doing single hand cuts with the deck. He practiced his lifts and his back-palms, and he contemplated his existence.

"Still practicing your sleight-of-hand type magic?" said Ahura as he appeared walking up silently behind Nicholas.

Nicholas was un-phased by his impromptu appearance and responded calmly, "There is a lot more than sleight-of-hand in this type of magic. I think you should know that the relationship between this "magic" and what I will call "Magick" as performed by the Magi has more in common than you may be aware."

Ahura looked at him and responded knowingly, with sarcasm, "Really?"

"Really," responded Nicholas with equivalent sarcasm. "In the same way that some martial arts instructors pay homage only to the outer aspect of the art to attract more customers who might please themselves in the transient satisfactions and the limelight of personal power, some sleight-of-hand artists only focus on the physical moves necessary to perform an effect. Thus, the students training in either art usually progress no farther than mere entertainment, since they have disregarded the necessary work towards inner growth."

Ahura sat down beside Nicholas at the edge of the dock and stared at the water. "Really?" he repeated again with less sarcasm, and even a little pride in his student's response.

"Really," responded Nicholas, and he continued, "I know now, even more so than before, that the performance of the magical art is not just a presentation of a multitude of tricks which display advanced sleight-of-hand or expensive illusions. The true presentation actually transcends the trick and becomes an almost spiritual event, which will cause the spectator to briefly believe in the non-rational explanation of observing the truly impossible. So this begs the question: What is truly impossible?"

"Hmm," said Ahura quietly under his breath. He continued to focus his attention towards the lake.

"The foundation of physical technique in either magic or martial arts is imperative for the practitioners but there is also an ontological basis, in both, which metaphorically, is the holistic earth on which the foundation rests. For the martial artist, it is the budo, or spiritual connection to the life force known as Ki, Chi, Prana, etcetera. For the magician, this spiritual connection can be found extensively in the origins of magic, and from the Shamans, the medicine men, and the Magi."

"But even in today's world, the true magician transcends the ordinary juggler by performing feats, which blur the line between imagination and reality by inspiring mystery, awe and a state of wonder in the observers. As Sam Sharpe said, 'Wonder is the key to the cosmos and magic helps fabricate that key.' Magic performed with an understanding of its potential impact, is indeed the quest of the true magician."

When Ahura spoke, his voice was calm, deep and as velvety as softened butter. "You have learned much in a very brief time. I commend you, Magus. However, there is and will be, much more to learn. Sure, there is a relationship between the martial arts practitioner and the true magician, even the sleight-of-hand artist, but more important is the relationship between them, and your beliefs, and true reality. Since the act of observation defines reality, and this reality is based on perception, if a spectator or anyone observes magic, whether it is at a magic show, or in life, does it really happen? That is the real question." He paused. "What if the observers truly believe, and more importantly, what if the magician truly believes?"

Nicholas understood the quandary.

Ahura continued, "These are the questions you will seek answers to, as you travel the path of the Magi."

"I can tell, these are going to be interesting times," responded Nicholas.

"The times will be what you make them," said Ahura.

"I understand," Nicholas paused, "completely."

Ahura continued, "One thing is certain though. There is still evil attempting to alter this perception. And there is still much to be done."

Nicholas pondered the thought and responded solemnly, "I know."

"And of course, there is still one other certainty," said Ahura with a slight smile.

"And what is that, my teacher?" asked Nicholas lightening up as he noticed the smile.

Ahura stared into the eyes of Nicholas, "You have a white shirt."

Nicholas responded as if he had anticipated the exercise, "Ah, but you see, there are no certainties anymore."

Nicholas then smiled and added, "I have a blue shirt."

Nicholas' shirt slowly morphed from white to blue.

Ahura looked at Nicholas and smiled, "Welcome to the world of the Magi."

He paused and his smile diminished as he continued more seriously, "However, I must remind you that although your shirt may have changed externally, internally you still have much more work. I expect to be traveling with you to the Cloister again at the beginning of next summer to continue your studies. This time, your stay will be much longer. There is much more for you to learn, and the time is now, for the Others will be building their opposing sect in parallel," he paused, "But you will prevail, Magus. You have done well."

Ahura picked up a pebble on the dock and threw it out into the water. They both watched the splash without speaking. The circular ripples grew away from the point of origin and began to travel across the lake.

Epilogue

There are some hundred billion galaxies, each with, on the average, a hundred billion stars. In all the galaxies there are perhaps as many planets as stars, ten billion million. In the face of such overpowering numbers, what is the likelihood that only one ordinary star, the Sun, is accompanied by an inhabited planet? Why should we, tucked away in some forgotten corner of the Cosmos, be so fortunate?

Carl Sagan

The road to Goldstone was 31 miles long. It began as a two-lane road peeling off in the desert from Route 15 between Barstow and Las Vegas and headed into even more desert and then, eventually, towards the barren, lonely mountains beyond. The terrain that encroached the road was occupied with sagebrush that in an after-life became tumbleweed, which then traveled the lands as ethereal spirits of the plant kingdom, and occasionally got trapped under passing cars. There was an intermittent century plant or Joshua tree but for the most part it was sage that pimpled the ground beside the road and beyond. However, even the sage began to grow sparse, as the pavement traveled deeper into the desert hills... They too felt the need to de-populate in such a remote area.

Traffic was non-existent except for the occasional flatbed truck that carried a tank or two to Fort Irwin, beyond the Goldstone Complex. It was at Fort Irwin where General Patton trained his troops. Bullet casings still riddled the sand beneath the podium where he used to speak.

The road was paralleled by a 12-inch high fence, which could have been a deterrent for inquisitive elves or hobbits but was there in fact to ensure the safety of the desert tortoise, an endangered species in the area. Tortoise sightings were to be reported immediately to the Fort Irwin Head Biologist in which case an Army platoon in a Humvee would rush to the site and move the tortoise even deeper into the desert. The intriguing assumption was that there was an even more remote area of desert. Besides the tortoise, the other primary life forms were the rattlesnakes, the lizards, the wild burros and the hawks. There were also shrimp, which actually lay dormant beneath the dry lakes, and when the once a year rain came, the lakes filled-up with water and the shrimp came alive. It is somewhat reminiscent of "Instant Coffee" except that this is "Instant Scampi." Life does in fact find a way to survive, even in this desolation.

After passing through the lone kiosk security for Fort Irwin and entering into barbed-wire territory, the road to Goldstone turned left.

The Goldstone Deep Space Complex was the desert home for the Western Hemisphere antennas providing communication links with all of the Deep Space (and some not so Deep Space) satellites from Voyager – on. The facilities were spread out over 68 square miles with areas known as Apollo, Venus, Mars and the Echo sites. In the barren hills around the facilities were petroglyphs from an unknown Native American tribe that abandoned the area over 4000 years ago. There was not much here then, and there is not much here now. Except for the 70-meter Mars dish and the other antennas and facilities, there would be no reason to be in these hills. So why were the natives here?

At Goldstone, lost amongst the test equipment racks for Venus, now used for Radio Astronomy Research and Development, a lone SETI rack sat. SETI (Search for Extra-Terrestrial Intelligence) had lost most of its funding back in the 1990's. The search for transmission waves from other areas of the galaxy using the multi-spectral capabilities of SETI was terminated. This rack however remained in perfect working order. It could monitor areas of space for a plethora of signals, and could then be used to search and define origins. There was just no funding. But no funding didn't necessarily deter the rogue engineer from flipping a switch or two on occasion just to see....to see... just maybe...

Beneath the light of a single desk lamp, alone in the Venus facility, ten miles from the next station, a network operations engineer sat running some calibration tests on his station for monitoring signals from Venus. He knew the test would take hours to run. Tired and trying to stay awake he walked outside into the darkness to look at the heavens. The stars above the desert filled the sky. Even the dark spaces between the stars were filled with shadow images of stars and galaxies beyond the visible. He couldn't help but wonder about life in the infinite universe; the potential for life seemed unlimited.

He decided to perform his nightly vigil of flipping the SETI rack on, partly for maintenance to make sure everything still worked, but mostly he wanted to do it out of curiosity. The rack switched on with a low hum and came to life. He configured the SUN workstation for monitoring the heavens in the direction of Jupiter and beyond. Mars too, was within the dish's receiving area. It was one of those rare conjunctions of the planets. A data-stream of numbers jogged across the screen. Everything seemed to be working and he left it on.

The data-stream then took a turn, a symmetric, non-random turn. A little red light illuminated and an audible beep occurred on the SETI Rack. It had found something. He rushed to the computer and tried to pinpoint the carrier. He thought, 'It must be something deep in space beyond the solar system.' The non-random binary code continued across the screen and he decided to check the Doppler readings on the transmission. The Doppler would verify any movement of the transmitting device, how far away it was, and how fast it was moving away from the antenna.

"This can't be right," he mumbled to himself.

The numbers showed that the transmission device was moving toward the Earth at a very rapid speed. All other transmissions from deep space moved away from the Earth since that was the direction they had been launched in.

"No, damn it, this can't be right," and he hit the side of the six-foot rack of equipment.

The screen jumped at the impact but the numbers did not change.

"Okay fine," he said as if giving in to appease a ridiculous theory. "Fine. Well then where the hell are you coming from?"

He tapped the keyboard a couple of times trying to interpret the new data on the screen.

He checked the numbers, and stared at the screen as he said quietly with confusion, "From Mars?"

ABOUT THE AUTHOR

Thomas Chilton Meseroll is currently a Director of Engineering i the Space & Intelligence sector of the aerospace industry. He was th Program Manager for NASA's Deep Space Network and a senic consultant for the U.S. Airforce Military Satellite Communications Win; He received a Patent Award from Hughes Space and Communications f theorizing a method for communicating with the past and the future usir satellites with quantum entangled particle communication devices. He h. a BS degree in Astrophysics from UCLA and an advanced degree Geophysics and Space Physics from the same institution.

He has been a martial arts practitioner for 35 years and is an expe in Okinawan weaponry.

He is a proud member of the Society of American Magicians, t International Brotherhood of Magicians, the Magic Collector's Associatio the Magic Circle in London, and the Academy of Magical Arts (T Magic Castle) and is known as "The Magus: Master of Martial Magic" f his incorporation of martial arts in magic. He has been performing mag around the USA for over forty years. In 2007 he won the Close-L Magician of the year for the Southern California Assembly of the Society American Magicians: An award won previously by Dai Vernon and Goshman.

He is also a skilled juggler.

He is a Pastor and has performed weddings for martial artists Japanese gardens, secret magical weddings at the Magic Castle, and o ceremony for an agent of the CIA.

He is a marathon runner, a bibliophile, a devoted husband a proud father of two.

WWW.MARTIALMAGICIAN.COM

The true artistry of Magic is in the concealment of the artistry that actually makes the Magic happen. Similarly, much of the effort in the composition of this novel is hidden. It is because of the support from some very important people behind the curtain that this story of Magic, Physics, and Spirituality has come to fruition, and I wish to thank them accordingly.

First and foremost, I owe a tremendous debt to my wife Jill, my daughter, Melina, and my son Trevor, for their support of this effort over the past fifteen years. They have taught me that real magic happens on a daily basis and that those of us who are fortunate enough to take note and appreciate even the smallest of miracles, will surely become richer, better people who are equipped with the potential for even more magic.

I owe a special thanks though to my wife Jill to whom I have dedicated this book. She has been my editor, my logician, and my confident through these many years of getting this effort on paper. She changes my reality for the better everyday.

I owe special thanks to two extraordinary people at the Magic Castle: To Milt Larsen the co-founder of the Castle, for creating this outstanding magical establishment, a true icon in the magic community, and secondly for allowing me to use the trademark name in my book. His dreams truly became a reality in the Castle and continue to evolve still to this day. And to Carol Marie, the Magic Castle Historian, who personally helped with the realism and the editing of the book in relationship to the history of the Castle and magic in general.

Chris Sereg who is writing the screenplay for the story has been a constant source of assistance in both the logistics and the visuals. I am sincerely grateful for his help, and very much hope that the screenplay becomes a successful movie in the future.

I owe a tremendous amount of credit to the magical inspiration of my mentors: Jeff McBride and Eugene Burger, who I am also fortunate to call friends. They bestow a sense of meaning to magical performance and they have taught me the true significance of Wonder in the field of conjuring.

My dear friend Kozak was a personal inspiration, as well a surprisingly synchronous teacher in the area of Quantum Physics. Although at the mathematical level, I was somewhat adept, he assisted in my understanding of the true meaning behind the implications.

I wish to thank Steve Nelson for his sobering wisdom on existence.

I have fond memories of Winter training at Seaside Shotokan and barefoot runs in the snow with the Lawrenceville Tang Soo Do karate club which remind me that I am indebted to Sensei Penny Ringwood and Grandmaster Seoung Eui Shin for my tutelage in martial arts. I believe wholeheartedly that Sensei Ringwood is one of the finest instructors of traditional Karate' Do teaching today, focusing not only on bujutsu and kata but also on budo: the Martial Way of Life.

Finally, I owe a debt of thanks to my parents Marie and Charles Meseroll, who have always supported my pursuits in life, which have indeed been varied and numerous.